U0095317

赖声强 主编

海上西厨房

Shanghai Western Cuisine

上海科技教育出版社

图书在版编目（CIP）数据

海上西厨房 / 赖声强主编. —上海 : 上海科技教育出版社，2010.8
ISBN 978-7-5428-5029-4

Ⅰ. ①海… Ⅱ. ①赖… Ⅲ. ①西餐—烹饪 Ⅳ. ①TS972.118

中国版本图书馆 CIP 数据核字 (2010) 第106817号

海上西厨房

主编 / 赖声强
摄影 / 李志成

责任编辑 / 王克平
装帧设计 / 刘　菲
出版发行 / 上海世纪出版股份有限公司
上海科技教育出版社
（上海冠生园路 393 号 邮政编码 200235）
网址 / www.ewen.cc　www.sste.com
经销 / 各地新华书店
印刷 / 上海中华印刷有限公司
开本 / 889 × 1194　1/16
印张 / 13.25
版次 / 2010 年 8 月第 1 版　2010 年 8 月第 1 次印刷
印数 / 1-3 700
书号 / ISBN 978-7-5428-5029-4/TS · 27
定价 / 80.00 元

序一

《海上西厨房》的出版是上海餐饮业近期出现的一件很有意义的事情。首先，请允许我代表上海餐饮业行业协会向参与写作的中外各位西菜名厨表示衷心的感谢。

上海是中国西餐的发源地。虽然今日之中国到处都有形形色色的西餐馆，但西餐进入中国，其实是 1840 年鸦片战争以后的事。当时的上海在一夕之间，突然从一个落后的小渔村变成了对外通商大埠，外国传教士和商人摩肩接踵而来，西餐就这样猝不及防地首先自上海登陆中国。然后，经过了一百多年的经营与改进，上海的西餐又在五花八门的各国西菜中，注入了中式烹饪的特色，创造出独树一帜的海上西菜。它既不同于各国的地道菜肴，又有别于中国其他地方的西菜，可称之为“海派西菜”而无愧。

“海派西菜”既不是“全盘西化”，也不是用西方食材、中式烹饪法所烧制的“中西大菜”或“番菜”，而是真正吸取了西菜精髓，并将其特点发扬光大，所逐渐形成的菜式流派。

现在上海已经成为中国最大的经济与文化中心城市之一。上海正继往开来，朝着建设国际化、现代化大城市的目标迅速前进。伴随着 2010 年世博会在上海的举行，全世界更是把目光聚焦于上海。上海的餐饮市场为了适应国际化的需要，呈现一派中西荟萃、百花齐放的局面。

由于欧美发达国家实行全球经济一体化的策略，其跨国公司的商务活动遍及全球，而西菜历来又是高级宾馆餐饮的主要品种，因此上海的西菜大厨近些年来，一方面在西餐馆秉承有历史积淀的各国西菜传统，一方面又在高端消费的中餐馆创新出许多有时代风貌的海派西菜，其中不乏国内外消费者都喜爱的美味佳肴。《海上西厨房》既可为我国的西菜厨师提高技艺和多方面的业务水准起到滋养作用，也可洋为中用，给中餐厨师开发新中餐提供创意。另外，该书还将有助于广大消费者增强品评西餐的品位。我相信《海上西厨房》的出版问世一定会得到专业厨师和普通读者的双重青睐。

上海餐饮行业协会名誉会长、研究员

何文剑

序二

西餐进入上海，要比进入北京早得多。早在清道光二十三年(公元 1843 年)上海开埠后，洋厨师就已远渡重洋来到各国领事馆，于是法式、英式、美式西菜陆续在上海滩的大码头登场。 现在，随着中国社会经济的飞速发展、国民生活水平的不断提高，西餐已融入中国人的生活。上海作为国际化大都市，海派气息浓郁，无疑是与西餐文化接轨最快速、最专业的地方。

上海的“红房子”、“德大”等著名西菜馆的沧桑典故，在上海人的记忆里有着历数不尽的故事，其西式菜肴全国闻名。新中国成立后被国家领导人夸奖为：“中国第一流的西餐馆”。但是，严格地讲它们已不是正宗的西菜，而融入不少上海元素，故被称为“海派西餐”。

上海作为一个相对来说缺乏历史和文化根基的现代都市，其立于不败之地的法宝便是顺应时势，不断求变、求新。只要是好的、有品质的，中西兼容。《海上西厨房》一书的出版发行正是这样一种海派餐饮文化的体现。《海上西厨房》一书汇集了上海西餐业界著名中外烹饪大师制作的具有代表性的经典西式菜点，选料考究、操作精细，代表了目前上海西菜制作的水平和发展方向。其中有许多是传统的经典菜肴，流传几十年甚至上百年。另外，本书编者不拘泥于传统，为适应上海餐饮市场国际化的需要，对新元素、新观念进行了大胆的尝试，作出不少创新，使其更能体现时尚潮流和现代人的饮食习惯和口味。因此，《海上西厨房》作为同行在制作西式菜肴时的借鉴与参考，有利于推动中国西餐业的不断发展，也十分有利于西餐厨师提高业务水准。同时，随着中国更加对外开放，各地的涉外酒店对西餐专业人才的需求也日渐高涨。《海上西厨房》或可成为高档酒店打造专业性、国际化西餐人才的一份培训教材。

我祝贺《海上西厨房》的出版发行！

中华职业学校

薛计勇

2010年 6 月

赖声强

光大国际大酒店行政副总厨、国家级西餐评委、国家级高级技师、国家职业技能鉴定考评员

目录

Mulu

刘荣基

上海巴黎春天大酒店行政总厨

目录

Mulu

罗 兰

上海锦沧文华大酒店行政总厨

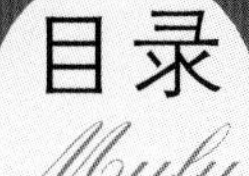

目录

Mulu

杰飞龙

上海东锦江索菲特大酒店行政总厨

目录

Mulu

新亚汤臣行政总厨、国家级高级技师、中国名厨、上海西餐专业委员会委员、国家级营养师、法国雅高集团比赛一等奖、美国厨艺学校进修

Mulu

赵希文

丽晟假日大酒店西餐行政总厨、技师、中国名厨、曾在悉尼喜来登酒店进修

目录

Mulu

李波杰

古井假日大酒店西餐总厨、高级技师、中国名厨、喜来登集团创新菜式金奖

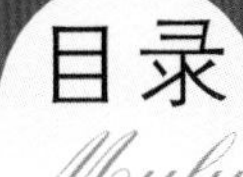

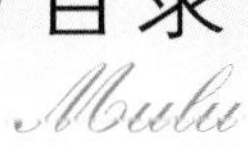

崔海荣

上海滨海皇家金煦大酒店西餐总厨、国家级技师、中国名厨、获得过喜来登集团第三届厨艺比赛三等奖

目录

Mulu

陈铭荣

正地豪生大酒店行政总厨、喜来登 B 级厨师证书、世界（中国）烹饪大师、曾获 FHC 烹饪大奖赛铜奖

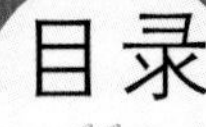

目录

Mulu

黄 健

宝钢集团宝山宾馆行政总厨、国家级高级技师、在日本东京第三回世界烹饪大赛获团体金奖、个人获得名菜名点等奖项

张雄林

宝山宾馆西菜厨房厨师长、国家级技师

目录

Mulu

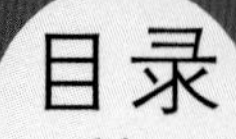

沈豪军

上海王宝和大酒店西餐厨师长、技师、中国名厨

目录

Mulu

邵 军

光大国际大酒店西餐主厨、国家级高级技师、中国名厨、曾获得喜来登酒店 B 级证书

目录

Mulu

郑纯涛

东方航空食品配餐有限公司食品技术部厨师长、国家级高级技师、曾获新中国60年上海餐饮业技术精英、万豪酒店餐饮培训管理证书、曾在新加坡文华酒店接受专业技术培训

目录

凌 云

中油日航大酒店餐饮部副总监、国家级高级技师、曾获得全国青年厨师赛优胜奖、新中国60年上海餐饮业技术精英称号

目录

Mulu

马光俊

上海皇冠假日酒店西餐总厨、国家级高级技师、曾获新中国60年上海餐饮业技术精英、被上海大酒店杂志评选为最佳推荐烹饪奖

目录

Mulu

莫自杰

上海艾福敦大酒店行政总厨、高级技师、中国名厨、曾获得厨艺设计大赛最佳推广奖、挪威海产品中国厨师烹饪大赛金奖

目录

Mulu

周剑伟

银河宾馆西餐厨师长、国家级高级技师、曾受训于意大利烹饪学校、美国农业协会附属烹饪学校

李伟强

杭州索菲特西湖大酒店西餐厨师长、国家级高级技师、中国西餐专业委员会委员、国家职业技能鉴定考评员、曾获2008年法国博古斯大赛中国区总冠军

徐高治

杭州华美达大酒店西餐总厨、浙江省西餐专业委员会常务委员、曾获得上海FHC国际烹饪艺术赛最高金奖

目录

Mulu

陆勤松

上海虹桥迎宾馆西厨房总厨、国家级高级技师、香港国际烹饪大赛银牌、曾在意大利托斯卡纳学院进修

目录

Mulu

1.海鲜鸭卷 Seafood Duck Roll

制作者 赖声强

原料 Ingredient

鸭胸 Duck Breast
风干火腿 Parma Ham
虾蓉 Minced Shrimp
蔬菜丁 Vegetable
鸡蛋 Eggs
香料 Spices
鹅肝酱 Foie Gras
柠檬汁 Lemon Juice
罗勒叶 Basil Leaves
橄榄油 Olive Oil
盐 Salt
胡椒 Pepper

制作 Proceed

(1) 整理鸭胸,用盐、胡椒、柠檬汁、香料腌制。

Marinate the duck breast with salt, pepper, lemon juice and spices.

(2) 将虾蓉、蔬菜丁、鹅肝酱、鸡蛋、香料拌匀。

Mix the minced shrimp, vegetables, foie gras, eggs, spices.

(3) 将(1)、(2)的原料卷成卷,外层用风干火腿包裹,进蒸箱蒸熟。

Take up the raw materials of (1), (2) into roll, wrapped with parma ham, then steam it.

(4) 装盘淋上汁水。

Arrange the plate,sprinked with sauce.

2. 酥皮鸡卷 Stuffing Chicken Roll

制作者 赖声强

原料 Ingredient

鸡胸肉 Chicken Breast
菠菜 Spinach
酥皮 Pastry
洋葱末 Onion
鲜菇 Mushroom
奶油 Cream
鸡蛋 Eggs
黄汁 Brown Sauce
黄油 Butter
白酒 White spirit
盐 Salt
胡椒 Pepper

制作 Proceed

(1) 鸡胸肉用盐、胡椒、白酒腌渍。菠菜口水后切成细末，用洋葱末、奶油炒透。

Marinate the chicken breast with salt, pepper and white spirit.Saute the chopped spinach,onion and cream.

(2) 将菠菜末用鸡胸肉包卷，再将酥皮包在外面，涂上蛋液，放入烤箱，烤至酥皮金黄。

Take up the chopped spinach into roll with chicken breast, wrapped with pastry, bust egg ,then put it in oven to roast.

(3) 将烤好的鸡卷装盆，淋上汁水。

Arrange the chicken roll on the plate and pour the sauce.

3. 清酒红石斑鱼 Sake Red Grouper

制作者 赖声强

原料 Ingredient

红石斑鱼 Red Grouper

娃娃菜 Baby Vegetables

芝麻菜 Arugula

土豆 Potatoes

清酒 Sake

辣椒汁 Chili Sauce

红原椒 Red Raw Pepper

柠檬汁 Lemon Juice

酸奶 Yogurt

金针菇 Golden Mushrooms

香脆薄饼 Crispy Pizza

制作 Proceed

(1) 红石斑鱼用清酒调味腌制。

Marinate the red grouper with sake seasoning.

(2) 娃娃菜、土豆用黄油、香料、白兰地酒煎熟，装盆，铺上芝麻叶。

Panfry the baby vegetables, potatoes with butter, spices and brandy. Arrange them on the plate, covered with arugula.

(3) 将煎熟的石斑鱼放在(2)上，淋上酸奶，放上金针菇，用辣椒汁配以薄饼装盆。

Put the Panfried grouper on (2), pour the yogurt, serve with golden mushrooms, crispy pizza and chili sauce.

4. 嫩煎海鲈鱼 Tender Fried Sea Bass

制作者 赖声强

原料 Ingredient

海鲈鱼 Sea Bass
菠菜 Spinach
小鲍鱼 Small Abalone
意大利节瓜 Italy Zucchini
白葡萄酒 White Wine
柠檬汁 Lemon Juice
胡椒 Pepper
刁草 Diao Grass
橄榄油 Olive Oil
罗勒叶 Basil Leaves
蒜泥 Mashed Garlic
番茄 Tomato

制作 Proceed

(1) 将海鲈鱼、小鲍鱼用白葡萄酒、柠檬汁、胡椒、盐、刁草、橄榄油、罗勒叶腌制。

Marinate the sea bass and small abalone with white wine, lemon juice, pepper, salt, diao grass, olive oil and basil leaves.

(2) 将菠菜用蒜泥、番茄翻炒。

Stir-fry the spinach with mashed garlic and tomato.

(3) 将腌制好的鲈鱼、小鲍鱼煎熟装盆，淋上新鲜番茄辣椒汁。

Put the Panfried sea bass and small abalone on the plate, serve with fresh tomato and chili sauce.

5. 鸡胸包榛子明虾 Chicken Rolls with Hazelnut and King Prawn

制作者 赖声强

原料 Ingredient

鸡胸 Chicken Breast
榛子 Hazelnut
明虾 King Prawn
瑞士小馄饨 Tortellini
蟹钳 Crab Pincer
彩椒丝 Julienne Peppers
迷迭香 Rosemary
奶油罗勒汁 Cream of Basil Sauce
白葡萄酒 White Wine
橄榄油 Olive Oil
盐 Salt
胡椒 Pepper

制作 Proceed

(1) 鸡胸用盐、胡椒和白葡萄酒腌渍,改刀待用;榛子打碎;明虾去壳、去筋。

Marinate the chicken breast with white wine, salt and pepper. Mash the hazelnut. Clean the king prawn.

(2) 鸡胸上铺一层打碎的榛子,中间放入明虾,卷成鸡卷,煮熟。

Make the chicken Roll with hazelnut and king prawn then put them in the water boiled to be done.

(3) 瑞士小馄饨煮熟后调味,用模具成型;蟹钳口水;彩椒丝用橄榄油拌匀。

Boil the tortellini to be done. Blanch the crab pincer. Mix julienne peppers with olive oil.

(4) 鸡胸卷改刀置于盘中,放上瑞士小馄饨等配菜,用迷迭香点缀,淋上奶油罗勒汁即可。

Put the chicken roll on plate, garnish with tortellini, rosemary, etc. Pour cream basil sauce.

6. 烤鸽腿配蓝莓汁 Roasted Pigeon Leg with Blue Berry Sauce

制作者 赖声强

原料 Ingredient

鸽腿 Pigeon Leg
北极贝 Shellfish
亚之竹 Artichoke
西兰花 Broccoli
中东小米 Couscous
彩椒粒 Chopped Peppers
黄瓜粒 Chopped Cucumber
蓝莓 Blue Berry
迷迭香 Rosemary
洋葱末 Chopped Onion
柠檬汁 Lemon Juice
雪梨酒 Sherry Wine
盐 Salt
胡椒 Pepper

制作 Proceed

(1) 将鸽腿用盐、胡椒腌渍,再放入烤箱内烤熟。

Marinate pigeon leg with salt and pepper then roast it to be done.

(2) 中东小米拌入彩椒粒、柠檬汁和黄瓜粒,煮熟后放入模具,置于盘中。

Boil couscous and mix it with chopped peppers, cucumber and lemon juice, put them in a mould on the plate.

(3) 洋葱末用黄油炒香,加入雪梨酒,浓缩后投入蓝莓,加入黄汁,再浓缩调味。

Saute chopped onion with butter, add sherry wine and inspissate the sauce. Add blue berry and brown sauce, inspissate and season.

(4) 亚之竹、西兰花用黄油炒熟并调味;北极贝改刀后过一下水。

Saute artichoke and broccoli, add seasoning. Soak shellfish.

(5) 将烤好的鸽腿装入盘中,淋上蓝莓汁,配上亚之竹等,以迷迭香等点缀即可。

Put the roasted pigeon leg on plate. Pour the blue berry sauce. Serve with artichoke and broccoli. Garnish with rosemary.

7. 煎小牛肉配雪梨酒汁 Grilled Veal Steak with Sherry Wine Sauce

制作者 赖声强

原料 Ingredient

小牛肉 Veal Steak
中东小米 Couscous
梨 Pear
各式水果 Fruits
红葡萄酒 Red Wine
白葡萄酒 White Wine
雪梨酒汁 Sherry Wine Sauce
玉桂粉 Cinnamon Powder
盐 Salt
胡椒 Pepper

制作 Proceed

(1) 将小牛肉用盐、胡椒和白葡萄酒腌渍一下;中东小米煮熟(做法参见第7页)置于模具中。

Marinate veal steak with salt, pepper and white wine. Steam couscous then put into mould.

(2) 梨去皮,用红葡萄酒加玉桂粉煮酥。

Boil pear peeled with red wine and cinnamon powder.

(3) 将小牛肉煎熟,装盘,配上中东小米、梨及各式水果,淋入雪梨酒汁即可。

Grill the veal steak to be done. Serve with couscous, pear and mixed fruit. Pour sherry wine sauce.

8. 双味水果冰糕 Two-flavor Fruit Sorbet

制作者 赖声强

原料 Ingredient

猕猴桃 Kiwi

黄桃 Peach

巧克力 Chocolate

摩司粉 Mousse Powder

奶油 Cream

蛋清 Egg White

糖圈 Sugar Ring

制作 Proceed

(1) 将新鲜猕猴桃、黄桃打碎,与慕斯粉、奶油、蛋清拌匀。

Blend the fresh kiwi and peach, mix with mousse powder, cream and egg white.

(2) 倒入模具内冷冻。

Frozen (1) into the mold.

(3) 取出装盘,配上糖圈、巧克力。

Arrange all the ingredients on the plate, serve with sugar ring and chocolate.

9. 煎烤兔排配波特酒汁 Roasted Rabbit Steak with Port Wine Sauce

作者 赖声强

原料 Ingredient

兔排 Rabbit Steak
兔骨 Rabbit Bone
土豆饼 Potato Cake
什菜(洋葱、胡萝卜和西芹) Mixed Vegetables
各式蔬菜 Vegetables
百里香 Thyme
罗勒叶 Basil Leaves
洋葱末 Chopped Onion
波特酒 Port Wine
番茄酱 Tomato Paste
盐 Salt
胡椒 Pepper

制作 Proceed

(1) 兔排用百里香、罗勒叶、盐和胡椒腌渍一下后卷成一圆柱,用竹签封口。用煎盘将兔排略煎后放入烤箱烤熟。

Marinate rabbit steak with thyme, basil leaves, salt and pepper. Wrap it to be roll.Panfry rabbit steak then put it in the oven to roast.

(2) 将兔骨炒透,加入什菜、番茄酱、波特酒和水,煮开,过滤,再加入波特酒和炒香的洋葱末,浓缩后调味,即成波特酒汁。

Saute rabbit bone, add mixed vegetables, tomato paste, port wine and water, boil and strain. Then add port wine and sauted onion, inspissate and season it.

(3) 各式蔬菜口水,用黄油炒熟并调味;土豆饼煎熟并改刀成三角形。

Blanch vegetables, saute with butter, then season. Fry potato cake and cut diagonal shape.

(4) 装盘时将土豆饼垫在下面,兔排拔出竹签后放在土豆饼上,配上炒好的蔬菜,淋上波特酒汁即可。

Put the potato cake on plate with rabbit steak on. Garnish with sauted vegetables and pour the port wine sauce.

10. 猪柳卷鳕鱼鹅肝 Loin Pork Roll with Cod and Goose

制作者 赖声强

原料 Ingredient

猪柳 Loin Pork
鳕鱼 Cod
鹅肝 Goose Liver
土豆丝 Sliced Potato
芦笋 Asparagus
紫菜 Laver
黑菌丝 Truffle
白葡萄酒 White Wine
雪梨酒汁 Shirley Wine Sauce
盐 Salt
胡椒 Pepper

制作 Proceed

(1) 将猪柳用盐、胡椒和白葡萄酒腌渍入味;鳕鱼打成泥并调味;鹅肝微煮。

Marinate loin pork with salt, pepper and white wine. Mash the cod and season it. Boil the goose liver.

(2) 将鳕鱼泥、鹅肝和紫菜卷入猪柳内,外面包上土豆丝,放入煎盘煎上色,再放进烤箱烤熟。

Wrap mashed cod, goose liver and laver with loin pork and sliced potato. Panfry it then put it in the oven to roast.

(3) 猪柳卷改刀,置于盘中,配上炒熟的芦笋及黑菌丝,淋上雪梨酒汁即可。

Put the pork roll on plate, serve with sauted asparagus and truffle. Pour the shirley wine sauce.

11. 龙虾芒果 Lobster Mango

制作者 刘永基

原料 Ingredient

波士顿龙虾 Boston Lobster
红圆椒丁 Chopped Red Bell Pepper
青圆椒丁 Chopped Green Bell Pepper
米饭 Steamed Rice
芒果 Mango
刁草 Dill
洋葱末 Chopped Onion
胡萝卜丝 Julienne Carrot
白萝卜丝 Turnip Juliennes
芒果汁 Mango Juice
白葡萄酒 White Wine
盐 Salt
胡椒 Pepper

制作 Proceed

(1) 把芒果肉用汤匙挖出，留下两口芒果壳备用。

Scoop out mango pulp and keep two half shell for later use.

(2) 龙虾用开水烫一下后把肉取出切片。

Blanch Boston lobster in hot water and take out meat on aside. Cut the meat into pieces.

(3) 炒香洋葱末，投入龙虾肉，加白葡萄酒和芒果汁煮 3 分钟，加入芒果肉后放在一口芒果壳内。

Stir-fry lobster meat with chopped onion, deglaze with white wine, add mango sauce and cook for 3 minutes. Put back mango pulp and place in one mango shell.

(4) 用黄油炒青圆椒丁、红圆椒丁和米饭，调味后放入另一口芒果壳内，用胡萝卜丝、白萝卜丝和刁草做装饰。

Stir-fry rice with butter and chopped green and red bell pepper and put into the other shell of mango. Garnish with julienne carrot, turnip juliennes and dill.

12. 兔肉批配羊肚菌 Rabbit Pate with Morels

制作者 刘永基

原料 Ingredient

兔肉 Rabbit Meat
猪肉 Pork
面皮 Pate Dough
猪肥膘 Pork Fat
芦笋 Asparagus
胡萝卜 Carrot
鸡蛋 Egg
羊肚菌 Morel Mushroom
混合生菜叶 Mixed Salad Leaves
洋葱 Onion
金巴利子 Cranberry
阿里根奴 Oregano
凝胶粉 Gelatin
奶油 Cream
盐 Salt
胡椒 Pepper

制作 Proceed

(1) 将猪肉、兔肉和猪肥膘用粉碎机搅成肉酱，混入奶油、鸡蛋、阿里根奴、煮熟的芦笋和胡萝卜丁，调味，备用。

Mince the pork, pork fat and rabbit meat with mincer, mix with cream, egg, cooked asparagus, carrot dice, oregano and seasoning.

(2) 把面皮贴在长方形铁模子内，填入混合肉料，再放上一层面皮，穿几个圆孔，放入烤箱烤，再拿出放凉。

Place pate dough in a rectangular form container neatly, then the mixture and cover on top a layer of pate dough and make several holes on top. Bake in a preheated oven. Take out and cool down.

(3) 用上汤把凝胶粉融化后灌入圆孔，再放入冰箱定形后装盘。

Melt gelatin with stock and pour inside through the hole. Put back in fridge until set.

(4) 把浸过水的羊肚菌用洋葱炒熟，调味；用等量的砂糖把金巴利子煮至酥透作伴汁；加上混合生菜叶，入盘装饰即可。

Stir-fry soaked morel mushroom with chopped onion and seasoning. Cook the cranberry with same amount of sugar until completely soft as sauce. Add mixed salad leaves as garnish.

13. 小龙虾色拉 Yabby Waldorf Salad

制作者 刘永基

原料 Ingredient

小龙虾 Yabby
青苹果 Green Apple
西芹 Celery
刁草 Dill
洋葱末 Chopped Onion
核桃仁 Walnut
蛋黄酱 Mayonnaise
辣茄汁 Tomato Chilli Sauce
盐 Salt
胡椒 Pepper

制作 Proceed

(1) 将小龙虾用调好味(加点什菜更好)的热开水煮熟,再浸入冰水使之爽脆,去壳(留数个不去壳的做装饰)。

Use hot and seasoned water (some mixed vegetable even better). Boil the yabbies until cook and put in ice-water for refreshment. Peel them but keep some unpeeled for garnish.

(2) 青苹果和西芹切粗丝后混入核桃仁、洋葱末和蛋黄酱做色拉底,淋点辣茄汁后,再把去壳的小龙虾肉放在汁面上,以刁草等做装饰即可。

Cut green apple and celery into strips and mix with chopped oinon, walnut and mayonnaise as a salad. Place tomato chilli sauce around the salad and top with the peeled yabbies. Put dill on top as garnish.

14. 鹌鹑清汤 Quail Consomme

制作者 刘永基

原料 Ingredient

芝士条 Cheese Straw
鹌鹑 Quail
黑菌 Truffle
鸡肉糜 Chicken Mince
盐 Salt
什菜(洋葱、胡萝卜和西芹) Mixed Vegetables
蛋清 Egg White
番茄酱 Tomato Paste
盐 Salt
胡椒 Pepper

制作 Proceed

(1) 将鹌鹑胸肉取出,部分煮熟以备装饰;黑菌切丝也备做装饰。

Cook some quail breast as garnish, slice truffle as garnish, too.

(2) 把鸡肉糜混合生鹌鹑胸肉、什菜、番茄酱和蛋清等,调味。

Mix chicken mince with raw quail breast, mix chopped vegetables, tomato paste, egg white and seasoning.

(3) 加入清水,用慢火煨,并不时捣一下,以防止焦底。烧开后用慢火再煨半小时,过滤并调味。

Add water into mixture and bring up slowly to make consomme. Stir occassionaly to prevent burnt. Boil then cook for another 1/2 hr with low heat, then strain and season.

(4) 放入芝士条、熟鹌鹑胸及黑菌丝装饰。

Put cheese straw, quail breast and truffle juliennes in as garnish.

15. 生蚝周打汤 Oyster Chowder

制作者 刘永基

原料 Ingredient

生蚝 Oyster
黄油 Butter
面粉 Flour
番茄丁 Chopped Tomato
什菜丁(洋葱、胡萝卜和西芹) Mixed Vegetables
刁草 Dill
奶油 Cream
上汤 Stock
白葡萄酒 White Wine
盐 Salt
胡椒 Pepper

制作 Proceed

(1) 生蚝取肉用黄油炒透,并烹入白葡萄酒。

Stire-fry oyster with butter, add white wine.

(2) 在汤煲中融化黄油,加入面粉捣匀,加入蚝肉、白葡萄酒和上汤。

Melt butter in a pan and mix in flour, add oyster, white wine and stock.

(3) 烧开后再煮20分钟,加入奶油,调味。

Bring to boil, cook for 20 minutes and add cream in it, season it.

(4) 用粉碎机将蚝肉和汤粉碎10秒钟。

Use a blender, put oyster in the soup and blend for 10 seconds.

(5) 什菜丁煮好,作为汤料,撒上刁草碎和番茄丁(也可用苏打饼干)即可上桌。

Use cooked and chopped onion, carrot, celery as garnish. Put chopped dill and tomato on top before served.

16. 鸡肉丸配明虾 Chicken Dumpling with Prawn

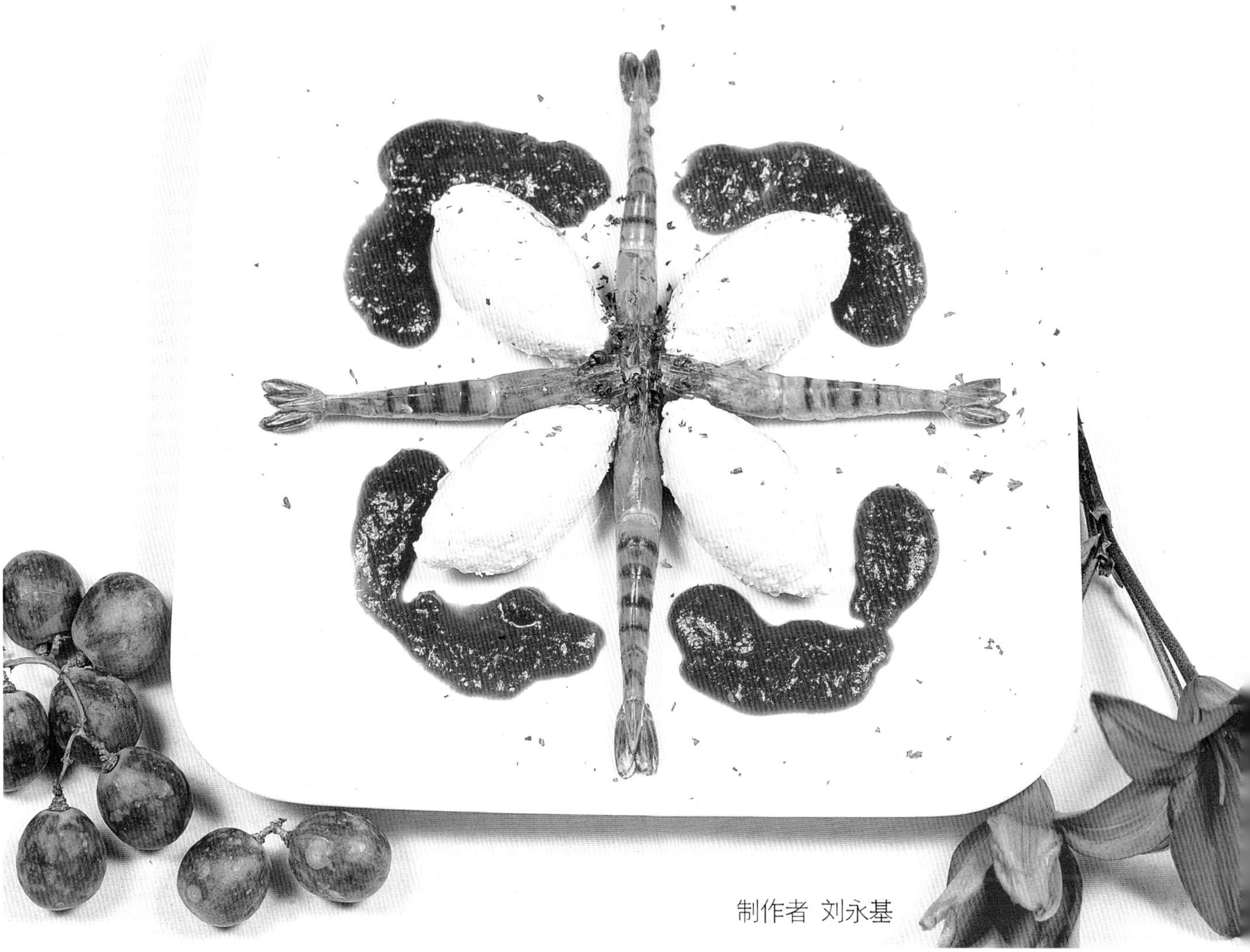

制作者 刘永基

原料 Ingredient

鸡肉糜 Minced Chicken Meat
明虾 Prawns
红甜椒 Red Bell Pepper
生粉 Corn Starch
荷兰芹末 Chopped Parsley
奶油 Cream
蛋清 Egg White
盐 Salt
胡椒 Pepper

制作 Proceed

(1) 把鸡肉糜和蛋清用粉碎机高速搅打 20 秒，再加入奶油慢速搅打 10 秒，调味。

Put minced chicken meat and egg white into blender, high speed for 20 seconds and pour in cream with low speed for 10 seconds, add seasoning.

(2) 用汤匙将鸡肉酱弄成丸状，放进开水烫至浮起。

Use spoon to make dumplings and poach in hot water until float up.

(3) 明虾用调好味的水煮熟做装饰。

Boil the prawns in seasoned water for garnish.

(4) 把红甜椒煮至酥透再粉碎，加入生粉并调味作汁。

Cook the red bell pepper until tender, blend with blender until liquid and thicken with corn starch and seasoning as sauce.

(5) 所有材料装盘，淋上红甜椒汁，撒上荷兰芹末。

Arrange all the ingredients on plate, pour red bell pepper sauce, sprinkle chopped parsley.

17. 三文鱼银鳕鱼配柠檬黄油汁 Salmon and Codfish with Lemon Butter Sauce

制作者 刘永基

原料 Ingredient

罗马生菜 Romaine Lettuce
银鳕鱼 Codfish
三文鱼 Salmon
柠檬黄油汁 Lemon Butter Sauce
柠檬汁 Lemon Juice
白葡萄酒 White Wine
白萝卜 Turnip
胡萝卜 Carrot
意大利节瓜 Zucchini
盐 Salt
胡椒 pepper

制作 Proceed

(1) 银鳕鱼、三文鱼先切厚方块，用盐、胡椒、白葡萄酒和柠檬汁腌渍入味，再把两种鱼叠起。

Cut codfish and salmon into cubes, marinate them with white wine, lemon juice, salt and pepper, then stap up together.

(2) 罗马生菜先用开水烫一下后把鱼包成方块，蒸 15 分钟后对角切，装盘。

Blanch romaine lettuce and wrap the fish into a squar piece. Steam for 15 minutes. Cut diagonal shape and put it on plate.

(3) 淋入柠檬黄油汁，将白萝卜、胡萝卜和意大利节瓜挖丸做装饰。

Pour lemon butter sauce, garnish with turnip, carrot and zucchini.

18. 鸭胸野菌汁 Duck Breast with Procini Sauce

制作者 刘永基

原料 Ingredient

鸭胸 Duck Breast
野菌(牛肝菌)Porcini
鸡蛋 Egg
菠菜 Spinach
胡萝卜 Carrot
白萝卜 Turnip
生粉 Corn Starch
黄汁 Brown Sauce
奶油 Cream
盐 Salt
胡椒 Pepper

制作 Proceed

(1) 煎熟调味好的鸭胸,然后批成片;野菌放入黄汁约烧 30 分钟作伴汁。

Panfry seasoned duck breast and sliced into pieces, cooked porcini with brown sauce for 30 minutes as sauce.

(2) 将菠菜、胡萝卜和白萝卜分别煮酥透,放入粉碎机打成糊状,分别加入蛋清、生粉、奶油、盐和胡椒,每种菜浆在杯模分层次约蒸 5 分钟。

Cook the spinach, carrot and turnip separately till tender. Blend with blender and add egg white, corn starch, cream, salt and pepper individually. Steam the vegetable mixture one at a time for 5 minutes in a dariol mould.

(3) 将鸭胸片和菜糕放好后浇上野菌汁,装饰即可。

Arrange vegetable mousse and duck breast slices on the plate and pour the porcini sauce.

19. 意大利烩牛膝 Ossobuco

制作者 刘永基

原料 Ingredient

牛膝骨 Veal Shank
胡萝卜 Chopped Carrot
洋葱 Onion
西芹 Celery
意大利节瓜 Zucchini
白萝卜 Turnip
面粉 Flour
橙皮 Orange Zest
藏茴香籽 Caraway Seed
黄汁 Brown Sauce
黄油 Butter
番茄酱 Tomato Paste
红葡萄酒 Red Wine
盐 Salt
胡椒 Pepper

制作 Proceed

(1) 先将牛膝骨两面煎至呈金黄色备用。

Fry veal shank to brown, put aside.

(2) 把切碎的洋葱、胡萝卜和西芹炒香,加入番茄酱、藏茴香籽和切碎的橙皮,5 分钟后加入面粉,略炒,再加入红葡萄酒。

Stir-fry chopped onion, carrot, celery, add tomato paste, caraway seed and orange zest. Put in flour after 5 minutes, deglaze with red wine.

(3) 把牛膝骨和黄汁加进去烧开,再用小火烩至牛膝骨酥透,调味后把汁水调至适当厚薄。

Put veal shank and brown sauce and bring to boil, simmer until veal shank is tender. Put seasoning and check consistance of sauce.

(4) 把胡萝卜、意大利节瓜和白萝卜切成宽面条状,用黄油炒好做装饰。

Cut carrot, zucchini and turnip into fettucine shape and stir-fry with butter as garnish.

20. 威灵顿牛柳 Beef Wellington

制作者 刘永基

原料 Ingredient

牛柳 Beef Tenderloin
酥皮 Puff Pastry
猪膘 Pork Fat
鸡肝 Chicken Liver
蘑菇 Mushroom
洋葱末 Chopped Onion
红酒汁 Red Wine Sauce
盐 Salt
胡椒 Pepper

制作 Proceed

(1) 将牛柳用盐、胡椒腌渍后煎至四边金黄。

Brown marinated beef tenderloin all side.

(2) 鸡肝和蘑菇加洋葱末炒至熟，调味后打至呈糊状，即成鸡肝酱。

Stir-fry chicken liver and mushroom with chopped onion until cooked. Season and mash as wrapping material.

(3) 将酥皮压薄，铺上猪膘，再放些鸡肝酱，最后把牛柳放在中间，卷成长条面包状。

Knee puff pastry and put sliced pork fat then liver mixtrues. Put browned beef tenderloin in middle and roll into a long bread shape.

(4) 将牛柳卷放入 160℃烤箱，烤至所需成熟度(如烤 45 分钟可达 5 成熟)。

Put in preheated oven at 160℃ and bake until it is cooked as your desire(45 minutes about medium).

(5) 用红酒汁伴食。

Serve with red wine sauce.

21. 小龙虾配红皮小土豆色拉 Poached Baby Lobster with Red Skin Potato Salad

制作者 罗兰

原料 Ingredient

小龙虾 Baby Lobster
红皮小土豆 Small Red Skin Potato
什菜 Vegetables
大葱 Leek
番茄 Tomato
芦笋片 Sliced Asparagus
黑橄榄片 Sliced Black Olive
蒜末 Chopped Garlic
香菜叶 Coriander leaves
小洋葱末 Chopped Spring Onion
荷兰芹碎 Chopped Parsley
芥末 Mustard
干白葡萄酒 Dry White Wine
蛋黄酱 Mayonnaise
黄油 Butter
红酒醋 Red Wine Vinegar
柠檬汁 Lemon Juice
鸡汤 Chicken Stock
黑胡椒 Black Pepper
盐 Salt
胡椒 Pepper

制作 Proceed

(1) 红皮小土豆洗净并煮至表皮柔软，切成小块，加入热鸡汤、番茄、黑橄榄片、小洋葱末、荷兰芹碎、芦笋片、芥末、蛋黄酱和红酒醋，煮至各料融合，调味后即成土豆色拉。

Wash and cook the small red skin potatoes until skin soft. Cut the potatoes into cubes, add chicken stock, tomatoes, etc. Mix well and season with salt and pepper.

(2) 用黄油将蒜末炒香，加入柠檬汁、荷兰芹碎和黑胡椒调味。

Fry the chopped garlic with butter, add lemon juice, chopped parsley and black pepper for seasoning.

(3) 将什菜、大葱和黑胡椒粒放入沸水中煮，同时加入干白葡萄酒和柠檬汁，煮至香味溢出，加入小龙虾略煮，确保熟透取出，对半切开，一半去壳。

Boil the water with all the vegetables, white wine, black pepper corns and lemon juice for minutes. Add the baby lobster and simmer for minutes to be nicely done. Remove lobster from the stock and cut in half, half take out of shell.

(4) 将土豆色拉装盘，小龙虾排放在适当位置，淋入蒜香黄油汁，并用新鲜的香菜叶点缀。

Arrange the potatoes salad on a plate, arrange the lobster nicely, top with garlic butter and decorate with fresh coriander leaves.

22. 特制番茄摩苏里拉芝士色拉 Insalata Caprese

制作者 罗兰

原料 Ingredient

番茄(去皮) Peeled Tomato
摩苏里拉芝士 Muzzarella Cheese
新鲜罗勒叶 Fresh Basil Leaves
混合生菜 Mixed Lettuces
烤松子 Roasted Pine Nuts
巴美臣芝士粉 Grated Parmesan Cheese
蒜末 Chopped Garlic
黑醋汁 Balsamico Vinegar
盐 Salt
胡椒 Pepper

制作 Proceed

(1) 将罗勒叶与蒜末加橄榄油混合,打碎,加入芝士粉,加盐、胡椒调味,即成罗勒酱。

Blend basil leaves, chopped garlic and olive oil, add grated parmesan cheese, salt and pepper. The basil paste is done.

(2) 把番茄和摩苏里拉芝士切成薄片,和罗勒叶叠成塔状,再用十字刀切成4份,装盘,用生菜点缀。

Cut tomatoes and mozzarella cheese in slices. Arrange tomatoes, mozzarella cheese and basil leaves to a tower then arrange the 4 pieces on a plate, decorate with mixed lettuces.

(3) 盘中淋入罗勒酱和黑醋汁,撒上烤松子,并用新鲜罗勒叶点缀。

Arrange the basil paste, the balsamico vinegar and the roasted pine nuts around the plate, use fresh basil leaves for final decoration.

23. 红甜椒茄子汤 Roasted Red Bell Pepper and Eggplant Soup

制作者 罗兰

原料 Ingredient

番茄块 Tomato Cubes
红甜椒 Red Bell Pepper
茄子 Eggplant
菠菜 Spinach
巴美臣芝士粉 Grated Parmesan Cheese
大葱末 Minced Leek
洋葱 Onion
蒜末 Chopped Garlic
红糖 Brown Sugar
橄榄油 Olive Oil
酸奶油 Sour Cream
奶油 Cooking Cream
鸡汤 Chicken Stock
盐 Salt
黑胡椒 Black Pepper

制作 Proceed

(1) 新鲜菠菜洗净、切细，拌入酸奶油，并用盐、黑胡椒调味。

Blend fresh spinach (blanched and finely chopped) with sour cream and season with salt and pepper.

(2) 把茄子、红甜椒、洋葱用油涂一层，烤至表皮易脱落，去皮，切成粒。

Brush eggplant, red pepper and onion with oil, then roast in the oven until the skin is easy to be removed. After peeling, cut the vegetables in equal cubes.

(3) 用橄榄油将大葱末、蒜末翻炒片刻，加入红糖搅拌，倒入茄子、红甜椒、番茄块和洋葱，再倒入鸡汤，用小火煨至熟透。

Fry minced leek and chopped garlic with olive oil for a few minutes then add the brown sugar and stir it. Add eggplant, red pepper, tomato cubes, onion and chicken stock then bring to boil. Simmer until all the vegetables are well cooked.

(4) 用粉碎机将汤搅拌，使汤浓缩，然后过滤，再重新加热，并加入奶油，加盐、黑胡椒调味，装盘后用芝士粉和菠菜酸奶油点缀。

Use a blender to blend the soup, inspissate to thicken then strain it. Reheat and add the cooking cream and season with salt and black pepper. Serve in bowl and garnish with grated cheese and spinach sour cream.

24. 藏红花椰奶青口汤 Mussel Coconut Cream Soup with Saffron

制作者 罗兰

原料 Ingredient

黑青口 Blue Shell Mussel
椰奶 Coconut Milk
各式蔬菜丝 Julienne Vegetables
蒜片 Sliced Garlic
小洋葱末 Chopped Spring Onion
香菜叶 Coriander Leaves
藏红花粉 Saffron Powder
干白葡萄酒 Dry White Wine
淡奶油 Whipped Cream
盐 Salt
胡椒 Pepper

制作 Proceed

(1) 把小洋葱末、蒜片、干白葡萄酒和藏红花粉放入小锅内烧开，再加黑青口略煮，直至所有的青口都开口，取出，部分肉壳分离。

Add chopped spring onions, sliced garlic, dry white wine and saffron powder in a small sauce pan and bring to boil. Add the blue shell mussels and simmer until all the mussels are open. Separate some mussel meats from the shells.

(2) 将椰奶加入小锅，慢慢煮沸并浓缩，再加入淡奶油并煮开，用盐、胡椒适当调味。

Add the coconut milk into sauce pan and bring to boil and inspissate. Add the whipped cream and bring to boil, season with salt and pepper.

(3) 把蔬菜丝放入汤碗中，青口肉排放在周围，并用带壳的青口点缀。

Set the julienne vegetables into a deep soup bowl, arrange the mussel meats around and decorate with the mussels with shell.

(4) 把小锅中的汤倒入粉碎机中搅拌，使汤面产生小泡沫，再倒入汤碗中，并用香菜叶点缀。

Pour the soup in the sauce pan into a blender and mix well so that the soup is lightly foamed up. Pour the soup into the soup bowl and decorate with coriander leaves.

25. 海鲜配蔬菜 Oyster and Scallop Medley with Vegetables

制作者 罗兰

原料 Ingredient

鲜蚝 Oyster
扇贝 Scallop
各式蔬菜 Vegetables
培根 Bacon
蛋黄 Egg Yolk
黑菌片 Sliced Black Truffle
炸蛋面 Deepfried Egg Noodles
混合香料 Mixed Herbs
香叶 Bay Leaves
蒜末 Chopped Garlic
洋葱末 Chopped Onion
朝和粉 Tempura Flour
番茄汁 Tomato Juice
白葡萄酒 White Wine
橄榄油 Olive Oil
柠檬汁 Lemon Juice
盐 Salt
胡椒 Pepper

制作 Proceed

(1) 把蛋黄、朝和粉和水调成糊状，将蚝肉滚上朝和粉，再与面糊混合，入油锅炸至呈金黄色。

Mix egg yolk, tempura flour with water to a paste. Turn oysters in flour then into paste and deepfry until golden brown.

(2) 扇贝加盐、胡椒、柠檬汁腌渍后煎至两面金黄(不必熟透)；各式蔬菜加橄榄油以微火烤至表皮金黄且柔软。

Season the scallops with salt, pepper and lemon juice and panfry until golden on both sides (not well done). Brush all the vegetables with olive oil and grill until golden brown and softened on low heat.

(3) 蒜末、培根、洋葱末用橄榄油□炒，加入香叶和白葡萄酒，浓缩一下，加入番茄汁和混合香料，煨烧片刻，过滤并调味。

Saute chopped garlic, onions and bacon in olive oil. Add bay leaves and white wine and inspissate. Add tomato juice and mixed herbs and simmer for minutes, strain and season.

(4) 将(3)的汁水淋在盘底，蚝、各式蔬菜、扇贝及蛋面摆放其上，用黑菌片等点缀。

Pour the tomato sauce on the plate, put the oysters, scallops, vegetables and egg noodles on it, decorate with sliced fresh black truffle, etc.

26. 烩鲜蛤配白酒汁 Stewed Clam with White Wine

制作者 罗兰

原料 Ingredient

鲜蛤 Fresh Clam
小龙虾 Baby Lobster
新西兰蛤贝(半壳)
New Zealand Mussel (Half Shell)
鲜虾 Fresh Prawn
蟹壳(□熟) Blanched Crab Shell
青红椒丝 Sliced Green-red Capsicum
小番茄 Cherry Tomato
小洋葱 Spring Onion
蒜末 Chopped Garlic
葱花 Minced shallot
香菜碎 Chopped Coriander
罗勒叶 Basil Leaves
白葡萄酒 White Wine
柠檬汁 Lemon Juice
黑胡椒 Black Pepper

制作 Proceed

(1) 将蒜末、葱花入油锅用温火翻炒至软,加入鲜蛤等海鲜、小番茄及白葡萄酒,焖烧到蛤熟透(壳全打开)。

Saute the chopped garlic and minced shallots over moderate heat until softened. Add cherry tomatoes, seafoods and white wine, cover and simmer until the seafoods is cooked (make sure the clams are all open).

(2) 加入小洋葱、香菜碎和罗勒叶翻炒,用黑胡椒、柠檬汁调味。

Add spring onions, chopped coriander and basil leaves then stir. Season with pepper and lemon juice.

(3) 将蛤连汁水装入汤碗,用蟹壳、罗勒叶和青红椒丝等装饰即可。

Serve in deep bowls and garnish with crab shell, basil leaves and sliced green-red capsicum.

27. 香煎鳎鱼配芒果牛油果酱 Baked Sole Fillet with Mango Avocado Relish

制作者 罗兰

原料 Ingredients

鳎鱼柳 Sole Fillet
芒果 Mango
牛油果 Avocado
红甜椒 Red Bell Pepper
菠菜 Spinach
茴香 Fennel
洋葱末 Chopped Onion
蒜末 Chopped Garlic
红花奶油汁 Saffron Sauce
橄榄油 Olive Oil
黄油 Butter
奶油番茄汁 Cream of Tomato Sauce
重奶油 Cooking Cream
白葡萄酒 White Wine
柠檬汁 Lemon Juice
盐 Salt
胡椒 Pepper

制作 Proceed

(1) 鳎鱼柳用盐、胡椒、蒜末和柠檬汁腌渍，用橄榄油煎至呈金黄色；茴香□水，切成角调味，用黄油翻炒至呈金黄色。

Season the sole fillet with salt, etc., and panfry in olive oil until golden brown. Blanch fennel and cut it to wedges, season and saute in butter until golden brown.

(2) 将芒果、牛油果、红甜椒切成丁，加入洋葱末、柠檬汁、橄榄油、盐和胡椒充分混合。

Cut the mango, avocado and red bell pepper in cubes, add chopped onion, lemon juice, olive oil, salt and pepper, mix fully.

(3) 用黄油把洋葱末、蒜末炒香，加入切碎的菠菜翻炒，再加入白葡萄酒和重奶油，炖煮并搅拌，汤浓稠时过滤并调味，即成奶油菠菜汁。

Fry chopped onions and garlic in butter, add chopped spinach and saute. Add white wine and cooking cream then bring to boil. Strain it then season.

(4) 将茴香角置于盘中央，上面放芒果牛油果酱和香煎鳎鱼，四周分别淋入奶油番茄汁、红花奶油汁和奶油菠菜汁。

Lay the fennel wedges in the center of the plate, top with avocado and mango relish, top with panfried sole fillet. Arrange the sauces around on the plate.

28. 意大利面配咖喱虾酱 Spaghetti with Curry Prawn Sauce

制作者 罗兰

原料 Ingredient

意大利面条 Spaghetti
虾尾 Prawn Tail
鹌鹑蛋(熟) Boiled Quail Egg
柠檬香叶 Kaffir Lime Leaves
香菜 Coriander
罗勒叶 Basil Leaves
椰奶 Coconut Milk
鱼露 Fish Sauce
红咖喱酱 Red Curry Paste
罗勒酱 Basil Paste
盐 Salt
胡椒 Pepper

制作 Proceed

(1) 将一半椰奶混入红咖喱酱中搅拌至汁水柔滑,再倒入剩下的椰奶及柠檬香叶,烧煮片刻,再加入鱼露,用中火煨一下。

Combine half coconut milk with red curry paste, mix to a smooth paste, add the remaining coconut milk and kaffir lime leaves and bring to boil. Add fish sauce and simmer on medium heat.

(2) 将虾尾放入酱料,煨至熟透,再加入香菜和罗勒叶并停止加热。

Add the prawn tails to the sauce and simmer until the prawn tails are cooked well. Add coriander and basil leaves and stop the heat.

(3) 将意大利面条放入盐水中煮至熟透,沥干,入煎锅,加入咖喱虾酱,用低火加热使之完全混合,调味后装入汤碗,用罗勒酱(做法参见第23页"特制番茄摩苏里拉芝士色拉")、鹌鹑蛋等装饰。

Cook the spaghetti in salted boiling water until well done. Drain it and put it into saucepan then add the curry prawn sauce mixture. Toss over low heat until well combined. Season to taste and serve into deep pasta bowls. Decorate with basil paste, quail eggs, etc.

29. 烤羊腓利和中东小米 Roasted Lamb Fillet with Couscous

制作者 罗兰

原料 Ingredient

羊腓利 Lamb Fillet

中东小米 Couscous

番茄 Tomato

玉米饼 Popadam

土豆片 Sliced Potatos

酸奶 Yogurt

薄荷叶 Mint Leaves

香菜 Coriander

小洋葱 Spring Onion

洋葱末 Chopped Onion

蒜末 Chopped Garlic

芥末 Mustard

罗勒叶 Basil Leaves

柠檬汁 Lemon Juice

橄榄油 Olive Oil

红酒汁 Red Wine Sauce

黄油 Butter

芒果酸奶油酱 Mango Chutney Sour Cream

盐 Salt

胡椒 Pepper

黑胡椒 Black Pepper

制作 Proceed

(1) 洋葱末、蒜末、芥末、柠檬汁、盐、黑胡椒和酸奶混合在一起，将羊腓利腌渍并入冰箱，腌好后扒至中等熟度。

Mix chopped onions, chopped garlic, mustard, lemon juice, salt, black pepper and yogurt to a paste and marinate the lamb fillet then put it in the refrigerator. Bake it until medium done.

(2) 将橄榄油和少许盐放入沸水中，加入中东小米，搅匀后关火，待中东小米膨胀后加入小洋葱、番茄、薄荷叶和香菜，最后加入黄油，搅拌均匀。

Boil the water with olive oil and salt, pour in the couscous and stir, then take off the fire. While the couscous swell, add sliced spring onions, tomato cubes, mint leaves and coriander then add butter and stir well.

(3) 将薄荷叶加酸奶和橄榄油混合，用粉碎机打碎，加盐、胡椒调味。

Add the mint leaves, yogurt and olive oil into blender and mix well into a smooth sauce, then season.

(4) 将酸奶薄荷汁及红酒汁淋入盘底，玉米饼、中东小米装盘，罗勒叶放在中东小米上，羊腓利对半切开放在罗勒叶上，用芒果酸奶油酱和炸土豆片等装饰。

Arrange the sauce, pupadum, couscous, basil leaves and lamb fillet. Decorate with mango chutney sour cream and deepfried potatos.

30. 煎牛排配黑菌汁 Grilled Beef Tenderloin with Black Truffle Sauce

制作者 罗兰

原料 Ingredient

牛柳 Beef Tenderloin
橄榄油 Olive Oil
盐 Salt
黑胡椒 Black Pepper
黑菌汁 Truffle Sauce
黄油 Butter
奶油 Cream
培根末 Chopped Bacon
迷迭香碎 Chopped Rosemary
洋葱末 Chopped Onion
栗子碎 Chopped Chestnut
土豆片(熟) Sliced Potatos (Boiled)
火腿片 Sliced Parma Ham
蘑菇 Button Mushroom
香菇 Shiitake Mushroom
蒜末 Chopped Garlic
鹅肝 Goose Liver
菠菜 Spinach
红葡萄酒 Red Wine
小洋葱 Spring Onion
烤蒜 Roasted Garlic

制作 Proceed

(1) 将蘑菇、香菇用橄榄油加蒜末翻炒至呈金黄色，用盐和黑胡椒调味。将牛柳边上切开，填入蘑菇等，再用火腿片包裹，并用牙签固定，根据口味腌制后煎烤两面。

Fry the mushrooms and garlic in olive oil until golden brown then season it.Cut the beef tenderloin from the side and stuffed with mushrooms and wrapped with the slices of parma ham, use a tooth pick to hold together. Season the beef tenderloin and grill on both sides.

(2) 将培根末、洋葱末、迷迭香碎和栗子碎用黄油翻炒，加入土豆片和奶油，慢慢煮沸，浓缩至奶油与所有原料融合在一起。

Saute chopped bacon, onion, rosemary and chestnut in butter. Add the sliced potatoes and cream then simmer, inspissate until the cream keep all the ingredients together.

(3) 菠菜用黄油清炒并调味，和牛柳、土豆色拉一起装盘。鹅肝用盐和黑胡椒腌渍，再用黄油煎至两面金黄(半熟即可)，放在牛柳上，淋入黑菌汁，小洋葱与烤蒜等用红葡萄酒烧制，用作点缀。

Saute the spinach with butter and season. Arrange on the plate top with beef tenderloin and potato salad. Panfry the goose liver in butter until golden brown on both sides. Put it onto the beef tenderloin and pour the truffle sauce. Cook the sliced spring onions and roasted garlic in red wine for garnish.

31. 生三文鱼和鳎鱼片 Carpaccio of Salmon and Sole

原料 Ingredient

新鲜三文鱼 Fresh Salmon

鳎鱼 Sole Fish

腌三文鱼 Marinated Salmon

紫菜 Laver

混合生菜 Mixed Lettuces

小番茄 Cherry Tomato

法式面包 Baguette

芦笋 Asparagus

罗勒叶 Basil Leaves

松仁 Pine Nuts

蒜末 Chopped Garlic

刁草 Dill

干番茄泥 Mashed Sun-dried Tomato

鱼子酱 Caviar

甜椒调料 Sweet Pepper Vinaigrette

酸奶油 Sour Cream

酱油浓汁 Thick Soya Sauce

橄榄油 Olive Oil

盐 Salt

胡椒 Pepper

制作者 杰飞龙

制作 Proceed

(1) 用新鲜三文鱼将紫菜及鳎鱼包卷起来，放于盘中，腌三文鱼裱上酸奶油，放置其旁。

Roll the laver and sole fish with fresh salmon. Put it on plate. Set the marinated salmon beside it and pour sour cream on.

(2) 将混合生菜、小番茄及口水后的芦笋摆放在盘子边缘，根据需要可浇上甜椒调料。

Arrange the mixed lettuces, cherry tomato and boiled asparagus at the edge of the plate and put sweet pepper vinaigrette on top as need.

(3) 将罗勒叶与蒜末加橄榄油混合，打碎，加入碾碎的松仁，加盐、胡椒调味，即成罗勒松仁沙司。

Blend basil leaves, chopped garlic and olive oil, add the grated pine nuts, salt and pepper.

(4) 将罗勒松仁沙司、酱油浓汁淋入盘中，并以抹上干番茄泥的法式面包、鱼子酱及刁草等装饰。

Pour the basil pesto sauce and thick soya sauce on plate, garnish with caviar, dill and baguette with mashed sun-dried tomato.

32. 米酒浸扇贝配五香牛油果 Rice Wine Marinated Scallops, Spiced Avocado

制作者 杰飞龙

原料 Ingredient

大蒜 Garlic
番茄 Tomato
红洋葱 Red Onion
橙肉 Orange Peeled
红椒 Red Capsicum
黄瓜 Cucumber
橄榄油 Olive Oil
雪梨酒醋 Sherry Vinegar
盐 Salt
卡宴辣椒 Cayenne Pepper
红辣椒 Red Chilli
柠檬汁 Lemon Juice
番茄汁 Tomato Sauce
青柠汁 Lime Juice
米酒醋 Rice Wine Vinegar
白醋 White Vinegar
腌生姜 Pickled Ginger
鱼露 Fish Sauce
胡椒 Pepper
黑胡椒 Black Pepper
扇贝 Scallops
牛油果 Avocado
鱼子酱 Caviar
香菜叶 Coriander Leaves

制作 Proceed

(1) 把青柠汁、米酒醋、腌生姜、鱼露和大量碾碎的黑胡椒调和在碗中，扇贝切成圆片，放入碗中腌渍。

Combine lime juice, rice wine vinegar, etc. in a bowl. Slice each scallop across the grain into discs. Add scallops to mixture for marinating.

(2) 将牛油果、红辣椒切成粒，用柠檬汁、盐、胡椒及香菜叶腌渍，再使之成形，装盘。将腌制的扇贝轻轻地叠放在牛油果上，并用香菜叶、鱼子酱装饰。

Dice the avocado and red chilli, then marinate with lemon juice, salt, pepper and coriander leaves. Shape a disc of avocado mixture in the center. Put marinated scallops, slightly overlapping, on top of spiced avocado. Garnish with coriander leaves and caviar.

(3) 将大蒜和番茄打碎，加入切碎的红洋葱、橙肉、红椒和黄瓜块，搅打均匀，同时放入橄榄油、柠檬汁、番茄汁和雪梨酒醋，混合后加盐和卡宴辣椒，冷藏后装盘，淋入橄榄油和白醋即可。

Place garlic and tomatoes in a blender. Add chopped onion, orange, red pepper and cucumber, blend until smooth. With machine running, drizzle in olive and lemon juice. Add tomato juice and sherry vinegar, mix and season with salt and cayenne pepper. Arrange them at the edge of the plate. Pour the olive oil and white vinegar.

33. 意大利美味拼盆 The Antipasti

制作者 杰飞龙

原料 Ingredient

小牛里脊肉 Veal Fillet
谷巴火腿 Coppa Ham
意大利萨拉米香肠 Italian Salami
番茄吐司 Brusceta
腌甜椒 Marinated Peppers
番茄 Tomato
摩苏里拉芝士 Mozzarella Cheese
巴美臣芝士 Parmesan Cheese
混合生菜 Mixed Lettuces
白萝卜丝 Julienne Radish
炸小章鱼 Fried Baby Octopus
水瓜柳 Capers
小鱼干 Sun-dried Fish
罗勒松仁沙司 Basil Pesto Sauce
金枪鱼汁 Tuna Sauce
意大利油醋汁 Italian Vinaigrette Dressing
盐 Salt
胡椒 Pepper

制作 Proceed

(1) 把小牛里脊肉用盐、胡椒腌渍,煮好后切成薄片,并在上面浇上金枪鱼汁(注意用听装金枪鱼打汁,不要太厚),用水瓜柳装饰。

Poach the marinated veal fillet and slice thin, top with the tuna sauce, garnish with capers.

(2) 把谷巴火腿和意大利萨拉米香肠切成薄片;把番茄去皮,和摩苏里拉芝士一起切成片,再叠在一起,并裱上罗勒松仁沙司(做法参见第 32 页)。

Slice the coppa ham and Italian salami. Slice peeled tomatoes and Mozzarella cheese, then overlap each other with the basil pesto sauce on the top.

(3) 将上述材料与番茄吐司、刨片的巴美臣芝士及腌甜椒一起摆盘,用混合生菜、小鱼干和炸小章鱼等装饰,淋入意大利油醋汁即可。

Arrange all the ingredients. Decorate with mixed lettuces, sun-dried fish and fried baby octopus. Pour the Italian vinaigrette dressing.

34. 轻煎胡椒金枪鱼 Seared Peppered Tuna

制作者 杰飞龙

原料 Ingredient

金枪鱼 Tuna
西洋菜(豆瓣菜) Watercress
豆芽 Bean Sprouts
粉丝 Rice Noodle
青椒 Green Capsicum
大蒜 Garlic
黑胡椒碎 Crushed Black Pepper
酱油浓汁 Thick Soya Sauce
橄榄油 Olive Oil
柠檬汁 Lemon Juice
盐 Salt
胡椒 Pepper

制作 Proceed

(1) 将金枪鱼用盐、胡椒和柠檬汁腌渍入味，再裹上黑胡椒碎，然后略煎，改刀装盘。

Marinate tuna with salt, pepper and lemon juice. Coat the tuna with the crushed black pepper and panfry it.

(2) 用西洋菜和豆芽拌和，与油炸的粉丝一起装盘。

Make a salad from the watercress and bean sprouts. Deep-fry the rice noodles and arrange on plate.

(3) 青椒、大蒜加橄榄油、盐和胡椒，混合后打碎，与酱油浓汁一起淋入盘中。

Blend the green capsicum, garlic, olive oil, salt and pepper. Pour it with thick soya sauce into plate.

35. 藏红花风味海鲜汤 Saffron Flavored Seafood Soup

制作者 杰飞龙

原料 Ingredient

各式蔬菜（胡萝卜、西芹等）Vegetables
各式海鲜（三文鱼、海鲈鱼、虾、鱿鱼等）Seafoods
番茄角 Tomato Wedge
京葱 Leek
藏红花粉 Saffron Powder
鱼汤 Fish Stock
白葡萄酒 White Wine
盐 Salt
胡椒 Pepper

制作 Proceed

(1) 各式蔬菜翻炒一下，然后加入鱼汤和藏红花粉，烧开。

Saute vegetables, add fish stock and saffron powder.

(2) 各式海鲜炒一下，然后烹入白葡萄酒，再加上述的蔬菜汤并调味。

Saute the seafoods, deglaze with white wine and add the stock, then season.

(3) 将海鲜汤装盘，并以番茄角和炸京葱等装饰。

Garnish with tomato wedge and fried leek.

36. 煎明虾配豆豉汁 Sauted King Prawns with Black Bean Sauce

制作者 杰飞龙

原料 Ingredient

带头明虾 King Prawn with Head
牛油果 Avocado
彩椒丝 Julienne Peppers
豆芽 Bean Sprouts
金针菇 Golden Mushrooms
番茄 Tomato
姜 Ginger
香菜 Coriander
红椒 Red Chilli
干葱末 Chopped Shallot
大蒜 Garlic
豆豉 Black Bean
橄榄油 Olive Oil
柠檬汁 Lemon Juice
鱼汤 Fish Stock
红葡萄酒 Red Wine
盐 Salt
胡椒 Pepper

制作 Proceed

(1) 将牛油果捣碎,与少量切碎的红椒及番茄混合成牛油果酱,用香菜末、柠檬汁、盐和胡椒调味。

Make a guacamole from the avocados, chili and tomatoes. Flavor with chopped coriander, lemon juice, salt and pepper.

(2) 把彩椒丝与金针菇、豆芽一起轻拌,并用盐、胡椒、柠檬汁和橄榄油调味。

Toss julienne peppers together with golden mushrooms, bean sprouts and season all with salt, pepper, lemon juice and olive oil.

(3) 将明虾用盐、胡椒及柠檬汁腌渍后煎至熟。生姜切薄片,用油炸。

Season the jumbo prawns with salt, pepper and lemon juice. Panfry it. Fry the thinly sliced ginger chips in oil.

(4) 将干葱末和大蒜口炒一下,加红葡萄酒、豆豉和鱼汤,烧开,直至豆豉酥,调味。

Saute the shallots and garlic. Deglaze with red wine, then add black beans and fish stock. Boil until the beans are tender, then season.

(5) 将明虾摆盘,淋入豆豉汁,并以炸姜片装饰。

Arrange all the ingredients, pour the sauce and garnish with ginger chips.

37. 鲂鱼柳包米纸 John Dory Fillet Wrapped in Rice Paper

制作者 杰飞龙

原料 Ingredient

鲂鱼柳 John Dory Fillet
鸡腿菇 Chicken Leg Mushroom
黑木耳 Jew´s-ear
各式蔬菜 Assorted Vegetables
土豆 Potato
藕片 Lotus Root
米纸 Rice Paper
红胡椒 Red Pepper
蒜末 Chopped Garlic
香菜末 Chopped Coriander
干葱 Shallot
柠檬汁 Lemon Juice
白葡萄酒 White Wine
鱼汤 Fish Stock
黄油 Butter
盐 Salt
胡椒 Pepper

制作 Proceed

(1) 口炒干葱和红胡椒，加入白葡萄酒和鱼汤，制作浓汁。

Saute shallots and red peppers, add white wine and fish stock to make the coulis.

(2) 将黑木耳和鸡腿菇加蒜末炒至软，加入香菜末并调味。

Saute jew´s-ears, add chicken leg mushrooms, add chopped coriander and seasoning.

(3) 鲂鱼柳用盐、胡椒和柠檬汁腌渍入味，将炒过的菌类放在上面，再用米纸包裹，放入铁盘煎至呈金黄色。

Marinate John Dory fillet with salt, pepper and lemon juice. Place the sauted mushrooms on the John Dory fillet and wrap in rice paper then panfry until golden brown.

(4) 用黄油翻炒各式蔬菜、土豆和藕片，调味。

Saute the vegetables, potatoes and lotus root. Season them.

(5) 把炒过的蔬菜等放在盆中，将煎过的鱼柳包放在上面，淋入浓汁即可。

Dress the vegetables, etc. on the plate, place the John Dory fillet on top and garnish with the coulis.

38. 炖羊腿配蔬菜 Braised Lamb Shank with Root Vegetables

制作者 杰飞龙

原料 Ingredient

羊腿 Lamb Shank
各式蔬菜丁 Diced Vegetables
防风根草片 Diced Parsnip
藕片 Lotus Root
红辣椒 Red Chilli
土豆片 Sliced Potato
百里香 Thyme
迷迭香 Rosemary
羊肉汁 Lamb Juice
盐 Salt
胡椒 Pepper

制作 Proceed

(1) 羊腿用盐、胡椒腌渍入味。

Marinate the lamb shank with salt and pepper.

(2) 翻炒各式蔬菜丁并加入羊肉汁，放入腌好的羊腿，入烤箱烤至肉熟，带汁装盘。

Saute the diced vegetables, then add the lamb juice and lamb shank. Braise them in the oven until tender. Put them on plate with juice.

(3) 防风根草片及藕片用油炸黄，百里香、迷迭香塞入红辣椒，与煎熟的土豆片分别装盘做装饰。

Deep-fry the diced parsnip and lotus root. Fill the red chilli with thyme and rosemary, and put it on plate with sliced potato fried.

39. 小牛排配茄子、土豆和羊肚菌汁 Veal Cutlet with Eggplant, Potato, and Morel Sauce

制作者 杰飞龙

原料 Ingredient

小牛排 Veal Cutlet
茄子 Eggplant
各式彩椒 Peppers
土豆 Potato
培根 Bacon
防风根草片 Parsnip Chips
荷兰芹 Parsley
巴美臣芝士 Parmesan Cheese
奶油 Cream
酸奶油 Sour Cream
羊肚菌汁 Morel Sauce
盐 Salt
胡椒 Pepper

制作 Proceed

(1) 各式彩椒切成丝，翻炒后调味。

Saute all the sliced peppers, then season.

(2) 把茄子一切二，调味后放入烤箱烘烤，取出装盘，在茄子上放炒过的彩椒。

Cut the eggplant in half and season, then bake in the oven and top with the peppers.

(3) 翻炒培根丁，加入切成末的荷兰芹。

Saute the diced bacon, and add chopped parsley.

(4) 烘烤整只土豆，然后一切为二，挖出土豆肉，加入奶油、酸奶油、荷兰芹末和培根丁，并调味，再加巴美臣芝士，烘烤成乡村土豆。

Bake the potato whole, then cut in half. Scoop out the potato and add the cream, sour cream, parsley, bacon, parmesan cheese and seasoning. Bake it.

(5) 小牛排用盐、胡椒腌渍入味，煎好，摆放在盘子内，用乡村土豆、油炸防风根草片装饰，旁边放茄子，最后浇上羊肚菌汁即可。

Panfry the veal cutlet marinated with salt and pepper, then arrange on the plate, garnished with farmer potato and fried parsnip chips. Put the eggplant on the side, add morel sauce.

40. 奖章小牛肉配各式蘑菇 Veal Medallion with Mushroom Varity

制作者 杰飞龙

原料 Ingredient

奖章小牛肉 Veal Medallion

各式菌菇 Mushrooms

各式绿叶蔬菜 Green Vegetables

甜土豆 Sweet Potato

黄油 Butter

波特酒芡汁 Port Wine Glaze

盐 Salt

胡椒 Pepper

制作 Proceed

(1) 将小牛肉依口味腌渍后煎熟。

Panfry the marinated veal medallions.

(2) 将各式菌菇及各式绿叶蔬菜炒熟并调味。

Saute all the mushrooms and green vegetables.

(3) 将甜土豆煮熟捣碎,拌入黄油并调味。

Mash the sweet potatoes with butter and seasoning.

(4) 所有材料装盘,淋入波特酒芡汁(做法可参考第10页"煎烤兔排配波特酒汁")即可。

Arrange all the ingredients. Pour the port wine glaze.

41. 烤扇贝 Baked Scallops

制作者 周亮

原料 Ingredient

扇贝 Scallop

混合香料 Mixed Herbs

鸡蛋黄 Egg Yolk

黄油 Butter

白葡萄酒 White Wine

盐 Salt

胡椒 Pepper

卵石 Scree

制作 Proceed

(1) 先用蛋黄、黄油、混合香料、白葡萄酒等做一份蛋黄黄油汁（注意在打蛋黄黄油汁时温度不能过高）。

Make an egg yolk and butter sauce first.

(2) 将扇贝表面涂上蛋黄黄油汁，放入烤箱内,烤至呈金黄色。

Paint it on the scallops surface, then put the scallops into the oven, bake until golden brown.

(3) 扇贝装入盘中,用卵石做装饰。

Put scallops on plate, garnish with scree.

42. 海鲜色拉 Seafoods Salad

制作者 周亮

原料 Ingredient

大龙虾 Lobster
带子 Scallop
虾仁 Shrimps
混合生菜 Mixed Lettuces
茴香 Fennel
橙 Orange
西柚 Grapefruit
荷兰芹碎 Chopped Parsley
黑醋汁 Balsamico Vinegar
盐 Salt
胡椒 Pepper

制作 Proceed

(1) 将各式海鲜□水,冷却后加盐、胡椒调味拌匀。

Blanch the seafoods, then season with salt and pepper.

(2) 将各式海鲜放入盘中,放上混合生菜、茴香、橙肉和西柚肉,淋上黑醋汁,撒上荷兰芹碎即可。

Put seafoods on plate then put mixed lettuces, fennel, orange pulp and grapefruit pulp on. Add the balsamico vinegar and chopped parsley.

43. 土豆饼配三文鱼和酸奶油 Potato Cake with Smoked Salmon and Sour Cream

制作者 周亮

原料 Ingredient

土豆 Potato
烟熏三文鱼 Smoked Salmon
红菜头 Beetroot
洋葱 Chopped Onion
培根 Chopped Bacon
酸奶油 Sour Cream
牛奶 Milk
荷兰芹末 Chopped Parsley
香料 Herb
盐 Salt
胡椒 Pepper

制作 Proceed

(1) 土豆煮酥,去皮碾成泥;将洋葱末、培根末炒熟,加牛奶,烧开后加入碾成泥的土豆,用盐、胡椒、荷兰芹末调味,制成土豆泥。

Boil potato then mash it. Saute chopped onion and bacon, add milk. After boiling, add mashed potatoes, season with salt, pepper and chopped parsley. The mashed potato is done.

(2) 土豆泥做成饼,煎黄,置于盘中。

Make potato cake then panfry it. Put it on plate.

(3) 在土豆饼上裱上酸奶油,烟熏三文鱼折成花放在酸奶油上。

Add the sour cream, smoked salmon.

(4) 用红菜头、香料做装饰。

Flavor with beetroot and herb.

44. 金枪鱼色拉 Tuna Salad

制作者 周亮

原料 Ingredient

金枪鱼 Tuna Fish
混合生菜 Mixed Lettuces
柠檬片 Sliced Lemon
柠檬汁 Lemon Juice
油醋汁 Vinaigrette Dressing
混合香料 Mixed Herbs
黑胡椒碎 Crushed Black Pepper
盐 Salt

制作 Proceed

(1) 金枪鱼用盐、柠檬汁腌渍，外层撒上混合香料和黑胡椒碎。

Marinate tuna fish with salt and lemon juice, sprinkle mixed herbs and crushed black pepper over it.

(2) 嫩煎金枪鱼，然后改刀装盘。

Tender panfry the tuna fish then put it on plate.

(3) 用混合生菜、柠檬片做装饰，淋上油醋汁即可。

Serve with mixed lettuces. Pour vinaigrette dressing on.

45. 三文鱼卷配色拉 Salmon Spring Roll with Mixed Salad

制作者 周亮

原料 Ingredient

三文鱼 Salmon Fish
春卷皮 Spring Roll Skin
紫菜 Laver
混合生菜 Mixed Lettuces
虾子 Shrimp Roe
橄榄油 Olive Oil
柠檬汁 Lemon Juice
盐 Salt
胡椒 Pepper

制作 Proceed

(1) 先将三文鱼用盐、胡椒和柠檬汁腌渍入味。

Marinate salmon fish with salt, pepper and lemon juice.

(2) 三文鱼用紫菜、春卷皮包裹，炸至半熟。

Wrapped the salmon fish in the laver and spring roll skin and deepfry till 50% cooked.

(3) 三文鱼卷装盘，配以混合生菜、虾子和橄榄油。

Put it on plate, serve with mixed lettuce, shrimp roe and olive oil.

46. 煎红鲷鱼配牛油果 Panfried Porgy with Avocado

制作者 周亮

原料 Ingredient

红鲷鱼 Porgy
牛油果 Avocado
番茄 Tomato
洋葱末 Chopped Onion
番茄汁 Tomato Sauce
柠檬汁 Lemon Juice
白葡萄酒 White Wine
盐 Salt
胡椒 Pepper

制作 Proceed

(1) 红鲷鱼用柠檬汁、白葡萄酒加盐、胡椒腌渍一下。
Marinate porgy with lemon juice, white wine, salt and pepper.

(2) 将红鲷鱼煎至熟，装盘。
Panfry the porgy to well cooked, then put it on plate.

(3) 盘中再放入切成丁的牛油果、番茄及洋葱末等，淋上调好味的番茄汁。
Add diced avocado, tomato and chopped onion, then add the tomato sauce seasoned.

47. 扒鸡胸配扁豆 Grilled Chicken Breast with Lentil Stew

制作者 周亮

原料 Ingredient

鸡胸 Chicken Breast

小扁豆 Lentil

各式甜椒 Bell Peppers

洋葱末 Chopped Onion

黑醋汁 Balsamico Vinegar

盐 Salt

胡椒 Pepper

制作 Proceed

(1) 将鸡胸用盐、胡椒腌渍，再扒至熟。

Grill the chicken breast marinated with salt and pepper till it is well cooked.

(2) 用切成粒的各式甜椒与小扁豆、洋葱末混在一起炒熟，调味。

Saute the chopped bell peppers and lentils mixed with chopped onion, then season them.

(3) 将小扁豆等置于盘中，鸡胸放在上面，淋入黑醋汁即可。

Put lentils, etc. on plate and chicken breast on it. Pour the balsamico vinegar on the top.

48. 烤羊排配蔬菜 Roasted Lamb Chop with Vegetables

制作者 周亮

原料 Ingredient

羊排 Lamb Chop

各式蔬菜(红椒、节瓜等)

Mixed Vegetables(red pepper, zucchini, etc.)

土豆 Potato

混合香料 Mixed Herbs

罗勒叶 Basil Leaves

橄榄油 Olive Oil

盐 Salt

胡椒 Pepper

制作 Proceed

(1) 将各式蔬菜、土豆用盐、胡椒、混合香料和橄榄油腌渍后扒熟。

Grill mixed vegetables and potatoes marinated with salt, pepper, mixed herbs and olive oil.

(2) 羊排用盐、胡椒腌渍后放入烤箱内烤至半熟。

Roast lamb chop marinated with salt and pepper till 50% cooked.

(3) 将羊排改刀装盘,配上各式蔬菜、土豆,将罗勒叶、混合香料、橄榄油、盐和胡椒混合打碎,淋上即可。

Put the roasted lamb chop on plate, with the vegetables and potatoes aside. Blend basil leaves, mixed herbs, olive oil, salt and pepper, pour it on plate.

49. 烟熏火腿包玉米饼 Polenta with Smoked Parma Ham

制作者 周亮

原料 Ingredient

烟熏火腿 Smoked Parma Ham
玉米粉 Polenta Powder
黑橄榄片 Sliced Black Olive
辣椒汁 Chili Sauce
荷兰芹末 Chopped Parsley
盐 Salt
胡椒 Pepper

制作 Proceed

(1) 水烧开,加入玉米粉、盐、胡椒,冷却后做成玉米饼,再切条。

Make the polenta cake with polenta powder, salt and pepper, then cut into bar.

(2) 玉米条包上烟熏火腿,煎黄,装盘,淋上辣椒汁,撒上黑橄榄片、荷兰芹末即可。

Wrap the bar with smoked parma ham and panfry it, then pour the chilli sauce on and sprinkle sliced black olive and chopped parsley.

50. 烤牛柳配豆芽 Beef Tenderloin with Bean Sprouts

制作者 周亮

原料 Ingredient

牛柳 Beef Tenderloin
豆芽 Bean Sprouts
各式甜椒 Bell Peppers
日式酱汁 Yakitory Sauce
黑胡椒碎 Crushed Black Pepper
百里香 Thyme
盐 Salt
胡椒 Pepper

制作 Proceed

(1) 将牛柳用盐、胡椒腌渍，滚上黑胡椒碎和百里香。

Marinate beef tenderloin with salt and pepper, sprinkle crushed black pepper and thyme.

(2) 将牛柳烤至半熟。

Grill the beef tenderloin till 50% cooked.

(3) 豆芽和各式甜椒丝炒熟，调味，垫入盘中，再放上牛柳，淋入日式酱汁即可。

Saute the bean sprouts and shredded bell peppers, season and put them on the plate, then put the beef tenderloin on. Pour the yakitory sauce.

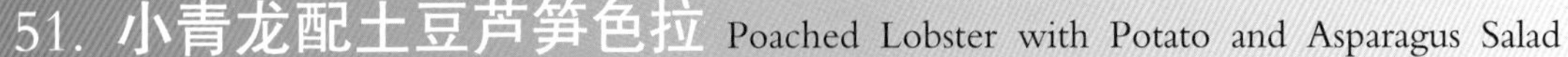

51. 小青龙配土豆芦笋色拉 Poached Lobster with Potato and Asparagus Salad

制作者 赵希文

原料 Ingredient

小青龙 Lobster
芦笋 Asparagus
土豆 Potato
青豆 Green Peas
胡萝卜丁 Carrot Dice
蛋黄酱 Mayonnaise
芥末汁 Mustard Sauce
盐 Salt
胡椒 Pepper

制作 Proceed

(1) 小青龙水煮至熟，放入冰箱冷却 1 小时，取出后龙虾肉切片叠放。

Boil the lobster to be done, then refrigerate it for an hour and slice the lobster meat.

(2) 芦笋修齐口水，围成圆柱状，土豆煮熟切粒，加入适量煮熟的青豆、胡萝卜丁、盐和胡椒，拌入芥末汁，镶入芦笋圆柱内。

Boil asparagus, diced potato, green peas, carrot dice with mustard sauce, salt and pepper.

(3) 所有材料装盘，淋入蛋黄酱，撒上青豆和胡萝卜丁做装饰。

Set all ingredients to plate, pour mayonnaise, garnish with green peas and carrot dice.

52. 香煎鹌鹑胸配蔬菜色拉 Panfried Quail Breast with Vegetable Salad

制作者 赵希文

原料 Ingredient

鹌鹑 Quail
鹌鹑蛋 Quail Egg
青红椒 Green-red Capsicum
芦笋 Asparagus
蒜末 Garlic
百里香 Thyme
芥末 Mustard
洋葱末 Chopped Onion
柠檬汁 Lemon Juice
红葡萄酒 Red Wine
橄榄油 Olive Oil
白酒醋 White Wine Vinegar
鸡汤 Chicken Stock
蛋黄酱 Mayonnaise
盐 Salt
胡椒 Pepper

制作 Proceed

(1) 鹌鹑洗净,取胸肉,用蒜末、柠檬汁、盐、胡椒、红葡萄酒和百里香腌渍,再煎至全熟。

Use the quail breast, marinate with garlic, lemon juice, salt, pepper, thyme and red wine, then grill it.

(2) 青红椒、芦笋修净,切成块状,□水,叠好装盘,再把鹌鹑肉放在上面。

Blanch the green-red capsicum and asparagus then put the quail breast on, set to plate.

(3) 将少许白酒醋和橄榄油、芥末、鸡汤、洋葱末、蒜末混合,放适量盐、胡椒调味,淋在菜上,以煮熟剖开的鹌鹑蛋及蛋黄酱装饰即可。

Mix white wine vinegar, olive oil, mustard, chopped onion, chicken stock., salt and pepper, pour it on plate, garnish with boiled quail egg.

53. 烟熏三文鱼花配青豆泥 Smoked Salmon with Green Peas Pulp

制作者 赵希文

原料 Ingredient

烟熏三文鱼 Smoked Salmon

青豆 Green Peas

鲜奶油 Cream

芝麻薄饼 Thin Pancake

柠檬汁 Lemon Juice

葱 Shallot

制作 Proceed

(1) 烟熏三文鱼切片,卷成花朵状。

Slice the smoked salmon and roll it to flower shape.

(2) 青豆□水,冷却后打成糊状,过滤,拌入柠檬汁,放少许鲜奶油并调味。

Boil the green peas then blend them and strain them. Put some cream, lemon juice and seasoning in.

(3) 将青豆泥铺于盘底,三文鱼放置盘中,以芝麻薄饼、葱和煮熟的青豆装饰即可。

Put the mashed green peas on plate, with salmon on it, garnish with thin pancake, shallot and boiled green peas.

54. 五彩羊腓利 Lamb Fillet with Tuna Sabayon

制作者 赵希文

原料 Ingredient

羊腓利 Lamb Fillet
各式甜椒 Bell Peppers
金枪鱼 Tuna Fish
黄瓜 Cucumber
芥末 Mustard
大蒜 Garlic
蛋黄酱 Mayonnaise
柠檬汁 Lemon Juice
盐 Salt
胡椒 Pepper

制作 Proceed

(1) 羊腓利用盐、胡椒、芥末调味,煎烤至七分熟。

Marinate lamb fillet with salt, pepper and mustard then grill it.

(2) 各式甜椒洗净,高温烤熟,去皮待用。

Roast bell peppers then peel them.

(3) 羊腓利切片装盘,中间缝隙用相应大小的甜椒填充。

Slice lamb fillet and put it on plate, fill with bell peppers.

(4) 金枪鱼加蛋黄酱、大蒜、柠檬汁混合,用粉碎机打匀,裱在羊腓利和甜椒上,盘边用黄瓜片装饰。

Blend tuna fish with mayonnaise, garlic and lemon juice, pour it on plate, garnish with sliced cucumber.

55. 黑椒金枪鱼配生菜 Grilled Peppered Tuna with Lettuces

制作者 赵希文

原料 Ingredient

金枪鱼柳 Tuna Fish Fillet
混合生菜 Mixed Lettuces
小番茄 Cherry Tomato
黑胡椒碎 Crushed Black Pepper
青柠汁 Green Lemon Juice
油醋汁 Vinaigrette Dressing
盐 Salt

制作 Proceed

(1) 金枪鱼柳四周滚上黑胡椒碎，用青柠汁腌渍，再煎至半熟。

Marinate tuna fish fillet with crushed black pepper and green lemon juice, then grill it to medium.

(2) 在盘子边缘围上混合生菜，中间放入煎好的鱼柳，淋入油醋汁，以盐棍和小番茄装饰。

Put tuna fish on plate, garnish with mixed lettuces, etc. Pour vinaigrette dressing.

56. 白灼鲈鱼柳配红花沙司 Boiled Seabass Fillet with Saffron Sauce

制作者 赵希文

原料 Ingredient

鲈鱼柳 Seabass Fillet
草虾 Shrimp
澳带 Scallop
各式蔬菜 Vegetables
洋葱 Onion
藏红花粉 Saffron Powder
黄油 Butter
鲜奶油 Cream
柠檬汁 Lemon Juice
白葡萄酒 White Wine
鱼汤 Fish Stock
盐 Salt
胡椒 Pepper

制作 Proceed

(1) 鲈鱼柳取中段,草虾去皮留尾,各式蔬菜修齐,□水待用。

Use the seabass fillet and shrimp, then boil them with vegetables.

(2) 取大只澳带,用柠檬汁、盐和胡椒腌渍后,放在扒炉上扒熟。

Marinate scallop with lemon juice, salt and pepper, then grill it.

(3) 各式蔬菜用黄油炒熟并调味,与鱼柳、草虾和澳带一起装盘。

Saute the vegetables with butter and seasoning, put it on plate with seabass fillet, etc.

(4) 将洋葱末□炒至香,加白葡萄酒、鱼汤和少许藏红花粉,烧至汤汁浓稠后,加入少许鲜奶油,调味后淋在盘中。

Saute the chopped onion, add white wine, fish stock and saffron powder. Inspissate it and add cream, then season it. Pour the sauce on plate.

57. 虾糕配浓缩鱼汁 Shrimp Cake with Fish Stock Sauce

制作者 赵希文

原料 Ingredient

虾仁 Shrimp
鱿鱼 Squid
草虾 Shrimp
洋葱 Onion
胡萝卜 Carrot
西芹 Celery
芝麻薄饼 Thin Pancake
鱼子酱 Caviar
奶油 Cream
白兰地酒 Brandy
鱼汤 Fish Stock
盐 Salt
胡椒 Pepper

制作 Proceed

(1) 将虾仁和鱿鱼用粉碎机粉碎成泥状，加少许奶油拌匀上浆，加白兰地酒、盐和胡椒调味。

Marinate mashed shrimp and squid with some cream, brandy, salt and pepper.

(2) 虾泥放入模具中，放进烤箱烤至熟，切成所需大小。

Put the mash into oven to be done. Then slice it.

(3) 将洋葱、胡萝卜、西芹切成小块，炒香，倒入鱼汤，浓缩，最后放入少许白兰地酒。

Saute the onion, carrot and celery, add fish stock, inspissate it, then add brandy.

(4) 将烤熟的虾糕与口水后的草虾装盘，淋上浓缩鱼汁，以芝麻薄饼、鱼子酱等装饰。

Put the shrimp cake and boiled shrimp on plate. Pour the fish stock sauce, garnish with thin pancake, caviar, etc.

58. 龙虾意大利菠菜面 Lobster and Spinach Noodle

制作者 赵希文

原料 Ingredient

龙虾 Lobster
意大利菠菜面 Spinach Noodle
白葡萄酒 White Wine
洋葱末 Chopped Onion
蒜末 Chopped Garlic
罗勒叶 Basil Leaves
鲜奶油 Cream
盐 Salt
胡椒 Pepper

制作 Proceed

(1) 龙虾留头、尾,中段剔出肉切片,用洋葱末、蒜末加少量白葡萄酒炒香;龙虾头和尾□水至熟。

Use the lobster meat and saute it with chopped onin, garlic and some white wine. Boil the head and tail of lobster.

(2) 意大利菠菜面煮至七分熟,将洋葱末和蒜末□炒至香,加入白葡萄酒、鲜奶油,烧开后再倒入意大利菠菜面,烧至汁水浓稠,调味并放入龙虾肉混合。

Boil the spinach noodle then stew it with chopped garlic, onion, some white wine and cream. Then season it and mix the lobster meat in.

(3) 龙虾头尾分置盘前后,中间倒入意大利菠菜面,以罗勒叶等点缀。

Put the mixed spinach noodle on plate, with the head and tail of lobster around, garnish with basil leaves.

59. 节瓜酿腓利 Zucchini Filled with Beef Fillet

制作者 赵希文

原料 Ingredient

意大利节瓜 Zucchini

牛腓利 Beef Fillet

羊肚菌 Morel

圆椒片 Sliced Bell Pepper

混合香料 Mixed Herbs

牛肉汤 Beef Stock

红葡萄酒 Red Wine

盐 Salt

胡椒 Pepper

制作 Proceed

(1) 取意大利节瓜中段,切厚片,挖去瓜瓤,□水待用。

Boil the zucchini.

(2) 牛腓利剔去血筋膜,用混合香料、盐、胡椒和红葡萄酒腌渍,再放在扒炉上扒至七分熟,改刀后酿入节瓜内,装盘。

Clean the beef fillet and marinate it with mixed herbs, salt, pepper and red wine. Then grill it to medium well. Fill the zucchini with the beef fillet. Put it on plate.

(3) 将羊肚菌放入牛肉汤中烩酥,使其饱含汤汁放在牛肉节瓜旁,以圆椒片装饰。

Stew morel with beef stock and put it aside, garnish with sliced bell pepper.

60. 烤羊排配蒜味红酒汁 Roasted Lamb Chop with Garlic Red Wine Sauce

制作者 赵希文

原料 Ingredient

羊排 Lamb Chop
各式蔬菜 Vegetables
蘑菇 Mushroom
洋葱 Onion
大蒜 Garlic
百里香 Thyme
鸡精 Chicken Powder
红葡萄酒 Red Wine
盐 Salt
胡椒 Pepper
黄汁 Brown Sauce

制作 Proceed

(1) 取羊排剔清血筋膜，用盐、胡椒及新鲜百里香腌渍入味。

Marinate lamb chop with salt, pepper and thyme.

(2) 羊排放在扒炉上煎扒上色，再放进烤箱烤熟。

Grill lamb chop then put it in the oven to be done.

(3) 洋葱和大蒜切碎、炒香，放入红葡萄酒和黄汁烧煮，待汁水浓稠后过滤，用盐、胡椒和鸡精调味。

Saute the chopped onion and garlic, then boil it with red wine and brown sauce. Inspissate and strain it, season with salt, pepper and chicken powder.

(4) 将羊排改刀装盘，配以炒熟并调味的各式蔬菜和蘑菇，淋入蒜味红酒汁，以百里香点缀。

Put the lamb chop on plate, serve with sauted vegetables and mushrooms. Pour the garlic red wine sauce, garnish with thyme.

61. 鲜贝色拉 Fresh Scallop Salad

制作者 李波杰

原料 Ingredient

鲜贝 Fresh Scallop
番茄丝 Julienne Tomato
混合生菜花 Salad Bouquet
罗勒酱 Basil Paste
白葡萄酒 White Wine
黄油 Butter
盐 Salt
胡椒 Pepper

制作 Proceed

(1) 鲜贝用盐、胡椒腌渍后煎制，烹入白葡萄酒，略煮，取出鲜贝，汁留用。

Marinate scallop with salt and pepper, then boil it with some white wine. Take scallop out and keep the juice.

(2) 鲜贝汁烧开，打入黄油并调味。

Heat up scallop juice then stir in some butter and seasoning.

(3) 装盘时，鲜贝汁如网状撒入盘中，放入番茄丝和鲜贝，用混合生菜花装饰，并用罗勒酱(做法参见第23页)点缀。

Pour the scallop sauce on the plate. Put julienne tomato and scallop on, garnish with salad bouquet and basil paste.

62. 特制烟熏三文鱼 Special Smoked Salmon

制作者 李波杰

原料 Ingredient

玉兰菜 Endive Lettuce
山羊芝士 Goat Cheese
蛋白 Egg White
烟熏三文鱼 Smoked Salmon
薄荷叶 Mint Leaves
柠檬肉 Lemon Pulp
红胡椒粒 Red Pepper
橙肉 Orange Pulp
柠檬汁 Lemon Juice
橄榄油 Olive Oil

制作 Proceed

(1) 取整片的玉兰菜，涂上山羊芝士，再平铺上一层薄荷叶，将烟熏三文鱼包住后卷成卷。

Take one piece of endive lettuce, smear goat cheese on it then cover a layer of mint leaf. Wrap the smoked salmon up.

(2) 蛋白煮熟，放入粉碎机打碎，一边打一边加入橄榄油和柠檬汁，取出后拌入柠檬肉。

Boil egg white then blend with olive oil and lemon juice, then mix some lemon pulp into it.

(3) 三文鱼卷装盘，把蛋白打成的汁浇在旁边，以红胡椒粒和橙肉装饰即可。

Set plate with the sauce around, garnish with red pepper and orange pulp.

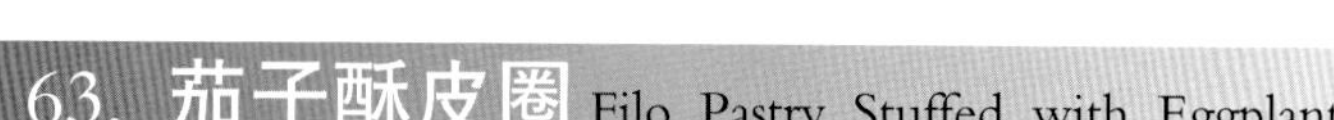

63. 茄子酥皮圈 Filo Pastry Stuffed with Eggplant

制作者 李波杰

原料 Ingredient

酥皮纸 Filo Pastry
茄子 Eggplant
生菜 Lettuce
橙肉 Orange Pulp
清黄油 Clear Butter
色拉油 Salad Oil
番茄汁 Tomato Sauce
盐 Salt
胡椒 Pepper

制作 Proceed

(1) 茄子连皮放在火上烤至熟,然后去皮取肉,打成泥,再拌入点茄子丁及盐、胡椒。

Grill eggplants on fire until it´s done then remove skin, mash it and mix some eggplant dice, salt and pepper in it.

(2) 用酥皮纸卷入茄子酱,表面刷上清黄油放入烤箱,烤至酥皮上色,用刀切去两边。

Roll it by filo pastry then brush some clear butter on surface, bake it until golden color, with two sides cut.

(3) 生菜加色拉油打成生菜油。

Blend lettuce and oil together.

(4) 装盘时垫入生菜丝和橙肉,酥皮卷放中间,四周淋上番茄汁和生菜油即可。

Put filo pastry rolls on the middle of plate underlaid with julienne lettuce and orange pulp, with some lettuce oil and tomato sauce around.

64. 鸡胸卷虾 Chicken Breast Roll with Shrimp

制作者 李波杰

原料 Ingredient

整鸡胸肉 Whole Chicken Breast
虾 Shrimp
菠菜 Spinach
巴美臣芝士 Parmesan Cheese
奶油 Cream
白兰地酒 Brandy
番茄丁 Tomato Dice
盐 Salt
胡椒 Pepper

制作 Proceed

(1) 鸡胸肉拍扁拍大，虾和菠菜□水。

Beat chicken breast until thin and big. Blanch shrimp and spinach.

(2) 鸡胸肉上放上虾和菠菜，撒点盐和胡椒，再用保鲜膜卷起，放入热水中煮至八分熟，捞出，去掉保鲜膜，煎成金黄色，用斜刀切成两半。

Put shrimp and spinach on chicken breast then season it and use plastic film roll it, then put in hot water, boil it until almost done. Remove plastic film and panfry chicken breast until golden color, cut to half.

(3) 巴美臣芝士、奶油、白兰地酒混在一起烧成奶酪汁并调味。

Melt parmesan cheese with brandy and cream, then season it.

(4) 装盘时鸡肉卷放中央，旁边淋上奶酪汁，用番茄丁等做装饰即可。

Set chicken breast on the plate, with parmesan cheese cream around, tomato dice for garnish.

65. 德式鹅肝酱 German Goose Liver Terrine

制作者 李波杰

原料 Ingredient

白蘑菇块 White Mushroom
德国咸猪手 German Pork Knuckle
鹅肝 Goose Liver
生菜花 Salad Bouquet
波特酒 Port Wine
桑果酱 Mulberry Jam
盐 Salt
胡椒 Pepper

制作 Proceed

(1) 鹅肝去皮、去筋，煮熟后碾成泥，调味；咸猪手煮熟，把肉取出撕成丝，肉皮与肉汁备用。

Move the skin and tendon of goose liver, boil the pork knuckle until it is done, keep the juice and skin and tear pork knuckle meat.

(2) 取一容器，放入一张保鲜膜，将鹅肝放入，铺上咸猪手肉丝，再铺上白蘑菇块。

Take a container cover a plastic film then put goose liver in, after put pork on it, put a layer of white mushroom on the top.

(3) 盖上咸猪手肉皮，浇入肉汁和波特酒，放入冰箱，24 小时后取出，切片装盘，用生菜花做装饰，配以桑果酱即可。

Cover it with pork knuckle´s skin, then pour pork knuckle´s juice and some port wine in. Keep in the fridge about 24 hours. Slice it and set to plate, garnish with salad bouquet and mulberry jam.

66. 鳕鱼土豆泥配芦笋和红花汁 Codfish and Potato Mush with Asparagus and Saffron Sauce

制作者 李波杰

原料 Ingredient

鳕鱼 Codfish
土豆 Potato
藏红花粉 Saffron Powder
各式蔬菜（芦笋等）Vegetables(Asparagus, etc.)
彩椒丝 Sliced Peppers
白葡萄酒 White Wine
柠檬汁 Lemon Juice
黄油 Butter
牛奶 Milk
盐 Salt
胡椒 Pepper

制作 Proceed

(1) 鳕鱼加牛奶、藏红花粉一起煮熟，鱼肉取出压成泥。
Poach codfish with saffron powder and milk until fish is done then mash it.

(2) 另取鳕鱼片用盐、胡椒、白葡萄酒和柠檬汁腌渍，卷入彩椒丝，煎熟。
Marinate another codfish with salt, pepper, white wine and lemon juice. Wrap the sliced peppers up, then panfry it.

(3) 土豆煮熟后压成泥，加入(1)的汁水，打匀，再拌入鱼泥，调味。
Boil potatoes then maush it with saffron milk. Put mashed fish in and season it.

(4) 芦笋等蔬菜□水后用黄油炒一下。
Blanch asparagus then saute it with butter.

(5) 装盘时，盘中放一个圆形模具，塞入土豆鱼泥，上面平铺一层芦笋，取下模具，配以鳕鱼卷等，旁边淋上浓缩的(1)的汁水即可。
Put the fish mash into a round mould, with the asparagus on top. Put the codfish roll aside, and pour the inspissated saffron milk for sauce.

67. 混合蘑菇卷 Mornay Bechamel Mix with Mushroom Crepe Gratin

制作者 李波杰

原料 Ingredient

各式菌菇 Mushrooms
面粉 Flour
鸡蛋 Egg
西兰花 Broccoli
奶油汁 Cream Sauce
牛奶 Milk
黄油 Butter
白兰地酒 Brandy
白葡萄酒 White Wine
巴美臣芝士 Parmesan Cheese
奶油 Cream
洋葱末 Chopped Onion
蒜末 Chopped Garlic
盐 Salt
胡椒 Pepper

制作 Proceed

(1) 牛奶、黄油、面粉和蛋液拌匀,放入不粘锅中加热做成圆饼。

Mix milk, butter, flour, egg together then panfry it to round shape.

(2) 把所有的菌菇都切成片,洋葱末和蒜末用黄油炒香后加入混合的菌菇一起炒,烹入白兰地酒并调味。

Slice all of mushroom then saute it with onion, garlic and brandy. Season it.

(3) 用饼包入炒好的菌菇,上面铺上奶油汁、蛋黄和巴美臣芝士的混合物,放入烤箱中烤上色,装盘。

Wrap the mushrooms by pancake, with the mixture of cream sauce, yolk and cheese on. Roast it to be well done. Then put it on plate.

(4) 西兰花加洋葱末口炒,加白葡萄酒和奶油,烧开并打碎,浓缩后调味,淋入盘中。

Saute the broccoli with chopped onion, add white wine and cream. Boil and blend it. Then inspissate and season it. Pour it on plate.

68. 煎橄榄鸡胸 Panfried Olive Crusted Chicken Breast

制作者 李波杰

原料 Ingredient

带皮带骨鸡胸 Whole Chicken Breast
黑橄榄 Black Olive
茴香 Fennel
胡萝卜 Carrot
甜椒 Bell Peppers
番茄丝(晒干) Sun-dried Tomato
洋葱末 Chopped Onion
蒜末 Chopped Garlic
番茄酱 Tomato Paste
鸡汤 Chicken Stock
盐 Salt
胡椒 Pepper

制作 Proceed

(1) 黑橄榄切碎,铺在鸡胸上,调味后将鸡胸煎上色,再放进烤箱烤熟。

Chop the black olive then sprinkle it on the chicken breast, then grill seasoned chicken breast and roast it until done.

(2) 茴香煮熟,加入番茄酱,放入粉碎机里打成泥并调味。

Boil fennel then blend it with tomato paste and seasoning.

(3) 甜椒入油锅炸一下取出,浸入冰水,再去皮。

Deepfry the bell pepper then put into ice water then remove skin.

(4) 将洋葱末和蒜末口炒一下,加入甜椒和鸡汤,开火烧至甜椒变软,调味后放入粉碎机里打碎,过滤后加入晒干的番茄丝。

Saute onion and garlic then put bell pepper and chicken stock in, after blend it well, strain it, and put some sun-dried tomatoes in.

(5) 把鸡胸切片后装盘,配以茴香泥和甜椒汁,用胡萝卜等装饰即可。

Slice chicken breast and put it on plate, serve with fennel mush and bell pepper sauce, garnish with carrot, etc.

69. 芥末羊柳 Mustard Seed Crusted Lamb Loin

制作者 李波杰

原料 Ingredient

羊柳 Lamb Loin
土豆 Potato
南瓜 Pumpkin
鸡蛋 Egg
芥末籽 Mustard Seed
鼠尾草 Sage
迷迭香 Rosemary
芝麻 Sesame
芒果丁 Mango Dice
糖 Sugar
八角 Anise
丁香 Clove
咖喱粉 Curry Powder
白葡萄酒 White Wine
白醋 White Vinegar
盐 Salt
胡椒 Pepper

制作 Proceed

(1) 羊柳用盐、胡椒腌渍,芥末籽和切碎的鼠尾草拌匀后撒在上面,再将羊柳煎至七分熟。

Marinate the lamb loin, sprinkle mustard seed and chopped sage on lamb loin then grill lamb loin until fine.

(2) 土豆去皮切片,拍上面粉,滚上蛋液和芝麻,炸熟。

Slice peeled potato then soak in flour, egg and sesame then deepfry it.

(3) 南瓜去皮、去籽,切片后扒熟。

Peel pumpkin seeded then grill it to be done.

(4) 芒果丁加糖、白葡萄酒、丁香、八角、咖喱粉和白醋,烧至汁水浓稠。

Heat up sugar, mango dice, white wine, clove, anise, curry powder and white vinegar together until thicken.

(5) 羊柳切开,与土豆片、南瓜片一起放入盘中,淋上(4)的汁水,以迷迭香等点缀即可。

Set potato and pumpkin on plate one by one, slice lamb loin with sauce, garnish with rosemary, etc.

70. 扒牛腓利 Cornmeal Cumin Rubbed Beef Fillet

制作者 李波杰

原料 Ingredient

牛腓利（里脊肉）Beef Fillet
土豆 Potato
玉米粒 Corn
番茄 Tomato
黄瓜 Cucumber
菜心 Bok Choy
孜然粉 Cumin Powder
红胡椒粒 Red Pepper
姜汁 Ginger Juice
椰奶 Coconut Milk
黄油 Butter
橄榄油 Olive Oil
盐 Salt
胡椒 Pepper

制作 Proceed

(1) 玉米粒煮熟后切碎，拌入孜然粉，然后在牛腓利上滚满，再将牛肉煎至七分熟。

Boil the corns then chop it and mix it into some cumin powder, rub beef fillet with it, grill beef fillet until fine.

(2) 土豆煮至酥，然后去皮压成泥，再加入椰奶，烧开调味，制成土豆泥。

Boil potato then mash it with coconut milk then season it.

(3) 菜心□水后用黄油炒一下，加入姜汁并调味；番茄和黄瓜切成丁，用橄榄油拌匀并调味。

Blanch bok choy then pour ginger juice and season it. Mix the diced tomato and cucumber with olive oil and seasoning.

(4) 将牛肉、土豆泥、菜心和番茄等装盘，撒上红胡椒粒装饰即可。

Set all ingredients to plate, garnish with red pepper.

71. 青瓜慕司 Cucumber Mousse

制作者 崔海荣

原料 Ingredient

青瓜(黄瓜)Cucumber
西瓜球 Watermelon Ball
哈密瓜球 Cantaloup Ball
橙肉 Orange Pulp
葡萄干 Raisins
香叶 Geranium
凝胶粉 Jelly Powder

制作 Proceed

(1) 将青瓜打碎。

Mince the cucumber.

(2) 凝胶粉加冷水，烧开，将打碎的青瓜放入，冷却后放入冰箱冻成型，装盘。

Add cold water in jelly powder, boil it. Put the minced cucumber in, then refrigerate it. At last put it on plate.

(3) 用西瓜球、香叶、哈密瓜球、橙肉、葡萄干装饰即可。

Garnish with watermelon ball, geranium, cantaloup ball, orange pulp and raisins.

72. 左口鱼卷 Halibut Roll

制作者 崔海荣

原料 Ingredient

左口鱼柳 Halibut Fillet
瑶柱肉 Minced Scollop
各式蔬菜 Vegetables
紫菜 Laver
蛋清 Egg White
柠檬汁 Lemon Juice
白葡萄酒 White Wine
红胡椒汁 Red Pepper Sauce
盐 Salt
胡椒 Pepper

制作 Proceed

(1) 左口鱼柳用盐、胡椒和柠檬汁腌渍一下。

Marinate halibut fillet with condiment.

(2) 瑶柱肉加盐、胡椒、白葡萄酒和蛋清搅打上劲。

Stir the minced scollop with salt, pepper, white wine and egg white.

(3) 用鱼柳将瑶柱肉和紫菜卷起,用保鲜膜包好,两头扎紧,放入沸水中煮熟。

Roll the minced scollop by halibut fillet, wrap with plastic film then boil to be done.

(4) 装盘,配炒熟的各式蔬菜,淋入红胡椒汁(可随意配置装饰)。

Garnish with sauted vegetables. Pour the red pepper sauce.

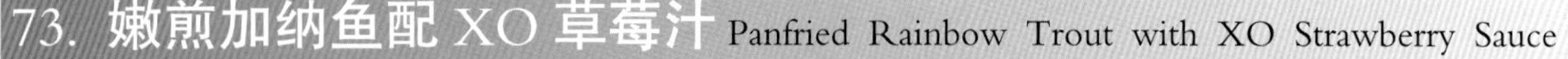

73. 嫩煎加纳鱼配 XO 草莓汁 Panfried Rainbow Trout with XO Strawberry Sauce

制作者 崔海荣

原料 Ingredient

加纳鱼柳 Rainbow Trout Fillet
各式蔬菜 Vegetables
XO 酒 XO Brandy
草莓 Strawberry
洋葱末 Chopped Onion
白葡萄酒 White Wine
柠檬汁 Lemon Juice
盐 Salt
胡椒 Pepper

制作 Proceed

(1) 加纳鱼柳用盐、胡椒、白葡萄酒和柠檬汁腌渍片刻，入煎盘煎熟。

Marinate rainbow trout fillet with salt, pepper, white wine and lemon juice, panfry it.

(2) 各式蔬菜用油炒熟并调味；洋葱末、草莓□炒后，加奶油，打碎并浓缩，再加入 XO 酒，调味后即成 XO 草莓汁。

Saute vegetables then season them. Saute chopped onion and strawberry, add cream. Blend it and inspissate it, add XO and seasoning.

(3) 加纳鱼柳装盘，淋上 XO 草莓汁，配以各式蔬菜即可。

Put the fish fillet on plate. Pour XO strawberry sauce, decorate with vegetables.

74. 煎明虾 Panfried King Prawn

制作者 崔海荣

原料 Ingredient

大明虾 King Prawn
各式蔬菜 Vegetables
红椒 Red Capsicum
刁草 Dill
洋葱末 Chopped Onion
白葡萄酒 White Wine
柠檬汁 Lemon Juice
盐 Salt
胡椒 Pepper

制作 Proceed

(1) 将大明虾用白葡萄酒、盐、胡椒和柠檬汁腌渍。

Marinate king prawn with white wine, salt, pepper and lemon juice.

(2) 用煎盘将明虾煎熟。

Panfry the king prawn.

(3) 将洋葱末与红椒口炒,加入白葡萄酒,烧开后打碎,浓缩并调味,即成红椒汁。

Saute the chopped onion and red capsicum, add white wine. Boil it and blend it. Inspissate and season it.

(4) 大明虾装盘,配以炒熟的各式蔬菜,淋入红椒汁,以刁草等点缀。

Put the king prawn on plate, serve with sauted vegetables. Pour the sauce, ganish with dill, etc.

75. 小牛肉卷配黑菌汁 Veal Roll with Truffle Sauce

制作者 崔海荣

原料 Ingredient

小牛柳 Veal Steak
各式蔬菜 Vegetables
百里香 Thyme
罗勒叶 Basil Leaves
混合香料 Mixed Herbs
黑菌汁 Truffle Sauce
红葡萄酒 Red Wine
盐 Salt
胡椒 Pepper

制作 Proceed

(1) 小牛柳批成厚片，用混合香料、盐、胡椒和红葡萄酒腌渍一下，然后将炒过的各式蔬菜与罗勒叶卷起，用竹签封口，放进烤箱烤熟。

Cut veal steak to slices, marinate with mixed herbs, salt, pepper and red wine. Roll it by sauted vegetables and bake it.

(2) 将烤熟的小牛肉切厚片，摆放盘内。

Slice the baked roll. Put it on plate.

(3) 淋上黑菌汁，以百里香及炒熟的各式蔬菜装饰。

Pour the truffle sauce, decorate to be done.

76. 烤鸡卷配鹅肝汁 Roasted Chicken Roll with Goose Liver Sauce

原料 Ingredient

鸡胸肉 Chicken Breast
海鲜泥(鲜虾等) Mashed Seafoods
鹅肝 Goose Liver
各式蔬菜 Vegetables
紫菜 Laver
混合香料 Mixed Herbs
洋葱末 Chopped Onion
黄汁 Brown Sauce
白葡萄酒 White Wine
红葡萄酒 Red Wine
奶油 Cream
盐 Salt
胡椒 Pepper

制作 Proceed

(1) 鸡胸肉用盐、胡椒、混合香料和白葡萄酒腌渍；海鲜泥调味后和紫菜一起用鸡胸肉卷起，略煎后放入烤箱烤熟。

Marinate chicken breast with salt, pepper, herbs and white wine. Stuff it with mashed seafoods and laver. Fry it to rare and grill it to well done.

(2) 鹅肝加洋葱末口炒，加入红葡萄酒和黄汁，烧开后打碎，再浓缩，加奶油、盐、胡椒，调味成鹅肝汁。

Saute the goose liver with chopped onion, add red wine and brown sauce. Boil and blend it. After inspissated, add cream, salt and pepper.

(3) 将烤好的鸡卷切成厚片，装入盘内，配以炒熟的各式蔬菜和鹅肝汁。

Cut the chicken roll into pieces. Put it on the plate, serve with sauted vegetables and goose liver sauce.

制作者 崔海荣

77. 煎牛排配干葱汁 Grilled Beef Tenderloin with Shallot Sauce

制作者 崔海荣

原料 Ingredient

牛柳 Beef Tenderloin
各式蔬菜 Vegetables
金针菇 Golden Mushroom
土豆球 Potato Ball
混合香料 Mixed Herbs
盐 Salt
胡椒 Pepper
红葡萄酒 Red Wine
干葱 Shallot
黄汁 Brown Sauce
帕尔玛火腿 Parma Ham

制作 Proceed

(1) 牛柳用盐、胡椒、混合香料和红葡萄酒略加腌渍，再用帕尔玛火腿卷起，煎至所需的成熟度。

Marinate beef tenderloin with salt, pepper and red wine then stuffed by parma ham. Fry it to be done.

(2) 将干葱炒香，加红葡萄酒和黄汁，烧开后调和，浓缩并调味，即成干葱汁。

Saute the shallot, add red wine and brown sauce. Boil and blend it, then inspissate and season it.

(3) 牛柳装盘，配上炒好的各式蔬菜、金针菇和炸熟的土豆球，淋上干葱汁即可。

Put the beef tenderloin on plate, serve with sauted vegetables, golden mushroom and deepfried potato ball. Pour the sauce .

78. 烤鸽腿 Roasted Pigeon Leg

制作者 崔海荣

原料 Ingredient

鸽腿 Pigeon Leg
葡萄干 Raisins
各式蔬菜 Vegetables
玉米 Corns
薄饼 Thin Pancake
酸奶油 Sour Cream
黄油 Butter
红葡萄酒 Red Wine
洋葱末 Chopped Onion
藏红花粉 Saffron Powder
混合香料 Mixed Herbs
黄汁 Brown Sauce
盐 Salt
胡椒 Pepper

制作 Proceed

(1) 鸽腿用混合香料、盐、胡椒和红葡萄酒腌渍,再用煎盘煎熟。

Marinate pigeon with mixed herbs, salt, pepper and red wine, then panfry it to be done.

(2) 各式蔬菜与玉米用黄油炒熟并调味;将酸奶油、藏红花粉、葡萄干拌匀,涂抹于薄饼上。

Saute the vegetables and corns with butter. Mix the sour cream, saffron powder and raisins to smear on the thin pancake.

(3) 将洋葱末、葡萄干口炒,加入红葡萄酒和黄汁,烧开后调和,过滤后浓缩并调味,即成葡萄干汁。

Saute the chopped onion and raisins, add red wine and brown sauce. Boil and blend it. Strain it then inspissate it and add seasoning.

(4) 鸽腿装盘,配上各式蔬菜、玉米与薄饼,淋上葡萄干汁即可。

Put the pigeon leg on plate, serve with vegetables, corns and thin cake. Pour the raisins sauce.

79. 煎鸭胸配马萨拉酒汁 Roasted Duck Breast with Marsala Sauce

制作者 崔海荣

原料 Ingredient

鸭胸 Duck Breast
玉米饼 Polenta
芦笋 Asparagus
红鱼子 Red Caviar
马萨拉酒汁 Marsala Sauce
盐 Salt
胡椒 Pepper

制作 Proceed

(1) 将鸭胸用盐、胡椒腌渍入味;玉米饼煎成金黄色。

Marinate duck breast with salt and pepper. Panfry the polenta.

(2) 将鸭胸煎上色,再烤熟。

Roast the duck breast then put it into oven to be done.

(3) 将烤好的鸭胸改刀装盘,配上炒熟的芦笋,淋上马萨拉酒汁(可以用雪梨酒和波特酒替代),以玉米饼及红鱼子装饰即可。

Cut the roasted duck breast into pieces, serve with sauted asparagus, polenta and red caviar. Pour the marsala sauce.

80. 羊柳鹅肝卷 Lamb Loin Roll with Goose Liver

制作者 崔海荣

原料 Ingredient

羊柳 Lamb Loin
鹅肝 Goose Liver
紫菜 Laver
各式蔬菜 Vegetables
迷迭香 Rosemary
百里香 Thyme
罗勒叶 Basil Leaves
阿里根奴 Oregano
红葡萄酒 Red Wine
白葡萄酒 White Wine
干姜汁 Ginger Sauce
盐 Salt
胡椒 Pepper

制作 Proceed

(1) 羊柳用盐、胡椒、红葡萄酒、迷迭香、百里香及阿里根奴腌渍。

Marinate lamb loin with salt, pepper, red wine, rosemary, thyme, and aregano.

(2) 鹅肝煮熟后碾成酱,加入百里香、罗勒叶、白葡萄酒、盐和胡椒拌匀。

Boil goose liver and make it to be catsup. Put the thyme, basil, white wine, salt and pepper in then blend it.

(3) 紫菜摊在台上,涂上鹅肝酱后将羊柳卷起,在煎盘中略煎后放进烤箱烤制。

Smear goose liver on laver then wrap the lamb loin up. Fry it to rare and grill it to be well done.

(4) 将羊柳卷切成厚片装盘,配上炒好的各式蔬菜及鹅肝酱等,淋入干姜汁。

Cut the lamb loin roll into pieces and put on the plate, serve with sauted vegetables and goose liver. Pour the ginger sauce.

81. 黑鱼子酱配煎饼 Black Caviar with Crispy Blini

制作者 陈铭荣

原料 Ingredient

黑鱼子酱 Black Caviar

黑面粉 Whole Wheat Flour

酵母 Yeast

鸡蛋 Egg

小干葱末 Chopped Shallot

荷兰芹末 Chopped Parsley

盐 Salt

胡椒 Pepper

制作 Proceed

(1) 将鸡蛋煮熟,分成蛋白、蛋黄,分别切碎。

Boil the eggs, divide egg white and egg yolk and chop it.

(2) 将黑面粉加盐、胡椒、酵母调匀,加少许牛奶,调成厚糊,煎成小饼。

Put seasoning in whole wheat flour, add a lot of milk to be paste. Make paste to small pancake.

(3) 将所有的材料摆盘即可。

Put all of product on dish.

82. 烟熏三文鱼烟熏鸭胸色拉 Smoked Salmon and Smoked Duck Breast, Mesclun Salad

制作者 陈铭荣

原料 Ingredient

烟熏三文鱼 Smoked Salmon
烟熏鸭胸 Smoked Duck Breast
生菜 Lettuce
意大利油醋汁 Italian Vinaigrette Dressing
黑橄榄泥 Black Olive Mash
辣根泥 Horseradish Mash

制作 Proceed

(1) 将烟熏三文鱼切片、修整齐，卷成花状；烟熏鸭胸批成薄片。

Roll sliced smoked salmon to flower shape, and slice smoked duck breast.

(2) 将生菜理齐卷成花状，放在盘中装饰，并淋上意大利油醋汁。

Make lettuce to flower shape and decorate dish. Put Italian vinaigrette dressing on dish.

(3) 将黑橄榄泥、辣根泥用小匙刮成橄榄形，摆盘装饰。

Make black olive mash and horseradish mash to olive shape by spoon.

83. 番茄芝士色拉 Tomato and Mozzarella Cheese Salad

制作者 陈铭荣

原料 Ingredient

番茄 Tomato
摩苏里拉芝士 Mozzarella Cheese
生菜 Lettuce
酥面皮 Filo Pastry
松子 Pine Nuts
罗勒叶 Basil Leaves
橄榄油 Olive Oil
盐 Salt
胡椒 Pepper

制作 Proceed

(1) 将番茄烫水去皮,切成菱形;将新鲜摩苏里拉芝士切成半圆形。

Put whole tomato in boiled water and out of skin, cut it to rhombus shape. Cut fresh mozzarella cheese to half round shape.

(2) 将罗勒叶、松子与橄榄油混合后打碎,调味即成罗勒松子汁。

Blend basil leaves and pine nuts with olive oil, then season to be paste.

(3) 将酥面皮做成小碗形盛器,略烤,装上生菜。

Make small bowl with filo pastary and put lettuce in.

(4) 将所有材料拼装入盘,淋入罗勒松子汁。

Arrange all ingredient nicely and pour the paste.

84. 玉兰菜西柚色拉 Endive and Grapefruit Salad

制作者 陈铭荣

原料 Ingredient

玉兰菜 Endive Lettuce

西柚 Grapefruit

小香葱末 Minced Chive

油醋汁 Vinegar Dressing

制作 Proceed

(1) 将玉兰菜洗净,修理整齐。

Wash endive lettuce and let it clean.

(2) 将西柚去皮、去筋,剔出肉,用油醋汁加小香葱末调成汁。

Cut off the skin of grapefruit. Put vinegar dressing, minced chive and grapefruit together and make sauce.

(3) 将玉兰菜排列整齐,中间叠起西柚肉,淋上汁水即可。

Put the grapefruit inside endive lettuce and pour the sauce.

85. 澳带青口贝串 Scallop and Mussel Skewer

制作者 陈铭荣

原料 Ingredient

澳带 Scallop
培根 Bacon
青口贝 Mussel
各式蔬菜 Vegetables
意大利双色面 Tagliatelle
红甜椒 Red Bell Pepper
大蒜 Garlic
鼠尾草 Sage
罗勒叶 Basil Leaves
干葱汁 Shallot Sauce
橄榄油 Olive Oil
黄油 Butter
盐 Salt
胡椒 Pepper

制作 Proceed

(1) 将澳带用培根包好,与青口贝一起串成串,煎熟。

Bacon roll scallop, add mussel to skewers and panfry them.

(2) 将各式蔬菜□水,用黄油炒熟,调味。

Blanch vegetables and fry them in butter then season them.

(3) 意大利双色面下熟,用橄榄油加蒜泥、盐、胡椒炒透,装入烤熟的红甜椒内。

Boil tagliatelle, then saute it with olive oil, chopped garlic, salt and pepper. Fill it in roasted red bell pepper.

(4) 将所有材料整齐摆放盘中,放入蒜头,淋上干葱汁(没有干葱可用洋葱替代),以罗勒叶、鼠尾草点缀即可。

Put all ingredients in dish and garnish it. At last, put garlic and shallot sauce on it, garnish with basil leaves and sage.

86. 法式蛙腿蜗牛 Frog Leg and Snail in French Style

制作者 陈铭荣

原料 Ingredient

蛙腿 Frog Leg

蜗牛 Snail

球形茴香 Fennel

面包 Bread

白葡萄酒 White Wine

茴香酒 Pernod

黄汁 Brown Sauce

混合香料 Mixed Herbs

盐 Salt

胡椒 Pepper

制作 Proceed

(1) 将球形茴香煮熟调味,切成扇形。

Cook the fennel, season and cut it to fan shape.

(2) 将蛙腿、蜗牛炒熟,加白葡萄酒、茴香酒去腥,再加入黄汁,调味。

Fry frog leg and snail, add white wine, pernod and brown sauce, then season.

(3) 所有材料装盘,用烤面包、混合香料装饰即可。

Put all ingredients in dish and garnish with roasted bread and mixed herbs.

87. 法式大明虾配姜味苹果汁 Tiger Prawn with Gingered Apple Chutney in French Style

制作者 陈铭荣

原料 Ingredient

大明虾 Tiger Prawn
土豆 Potato
生姜丝 Sliced Ginger
苹果 Apple
红糖 Brown Sugar
碎葡萄干 Chopped Raisin
咖喱汁 Curry Sauce
各式蔬菜 Vegetables
牛奶 Milk
黄油 Butter
盐 Salt
胡椒 Pepper
柠檬汁 Lemon Juice

制作 Proceed

(1) 将大明虾用盐、胡椒、柠檬汁腌透,煎熟装盘。

Fry marinated tiger prawn. Put it in dish.

(2) 将土豆煮熟,碾成泥,放入烧开的牛奶,加盐、胡椒,调成土豆泥,再裱成花朵做装饰。

Boil potato and make it to mash mixed with boiled milk, salt and pepper. Make potato mash to flower shape for garnish.

(3) 将各式蔬菜用黄油炒熟,调味。

Saute vegetables with butter and seasoning.

(4) 将姜丝、苹果切成小粒,加红糖、咖喱汁、碎葡萄干,制成姜味苹果汁,淋在大明虾旁,配以各式蔬菜即可。

Slice ginger and apple to dices, add brown sugar, curry sauce, chopped raisin and make all to gingered apple sauce. Put the sauce and vegetables in dish to garnish tiger prawn.

88. 法式牛肉塞鹅肝 Grilled Beef Tenderloin with Goose Liver in French Style

制作者 陈铭荣

原料 Ingredient

牛柳 Beef Tenderloin
鹅肝 Goose Liver
各式蔬菜 Vegetables
蘑菇 Mushroom
小胡萝卜 Baby Carrot
土豆饼 Potato Cake
小茴香 Cumin
生姜末 Minced Ginger
甜芥末 Sweet Mustard
小干葱末 Minced Shallot
黄油 Butter
牛肉汤 Beef Stock
盐 Salt
胡椒 Pepper

制作 Proceed

(1) 将鹅肝用盐、胡椒腌渍后煎熟。

Fry goose liver marinated with salt and pepper.

(2) 将牛柳调味后煎成半熟,在中间用刀开口,夹入鹅肝,装盘。

Fry marinated beef tenderloin, cut a slot and insert fried goose liver in. Put it in dish.

(3) 将小干葱末、生姜末炒香,加入甜芥末、牛肉汤,制成姜味甜芥末汁。

Fry minced shallot and minced ginger, add beef stock and gingered sweet mustard.

(4) 将各式蔬菜与蘑菇口水,用黄油炒熟并调味;小胡萝卜用小茴香加水煮熟;土豆饼煎熟。

Blanch vegetables, fry it in butter. Boil baby carrot with cumin. Fry potato cake.

(5) 所有材料装盘,淋入姜味甜芥末汁即可。

Put all ingrdients cooked in dish with the sauce.

89. 芝士菠菜鸡肉卷 Chicken Breast Roll with Cheese and Spinach

制作者 陈铭荣

原料 Ingredient

鸡胸 Chicken Breast
芝士 Cheese
菠菜 Spinach
各式蔬菜 Vegetables
双色面 Tagliatelle
蘑菇汁 Mushroom Sauce
罗勒叶 Basil Leaves
黄油 Butter
盐 Salt
胡椒 Pepper

制作 Proceed

(1) 将鸡胸用盐、胡椒腌渍后批成薄片,里面包上芝士和菠菜,卷成圆卷,煎上色,放进烤箱烤熟。

Slice chicken breast marinated with salt and pepper, insert cheese and spinach and roll it. Bake it to brown and roast it.

(2) 将鸡胸卷斜切成段,使部分芝士流出。

Cut chicken breast to pieces, let cheese can be seen.

(3) 将双色面下熟,用黄油炒透;各式蔬菜用黄油炒熟并调味。

Fry tagliatelle and vegetables in butter.

(4) 所有材料装盘,淋入蘑菇汁,并用罗勒叶装饰即可。

Put all ingredients in dish with mushroom sauce and garnish with basil leaves.

90. 岩石烧烤 Hot Rock

制作者 陈铭荣

原料 Ingredient

牛柳 Beef Tenderloin
牛肉眼 Beef Rib Eye
西冷牛肉 Beef Sirloin
猪排 Pork Chop
羊排 Lamb Chop
鲜鱼柳 Fresh Fish Fillet
大明虾 Tiger Prawn
各式蔬菜 Vegetables
大蒜黄油汁 Garlic Butter Sauce
黑胡椒汁 Black Pepper Sauce
BBQ 汁 BBQ Sauce
优质岩石 Rock Stone

制作 Proceed

(1) 将优质岩石放入高温的烤箱内烤数小时。

Put rock stone in high temperature bakery oven for several hours.

(2) 将牛柳等主料(任选)调味后放入盘内,与各式蔬菜一起逐一放在火烫的岩石上烧烤,佐以大蒜黄油汁(用蒜泥、黄油、李派林、白兰地酒、荷兰芹末混合而成)等调料。

Season all ingredients, and put one by one on the heat rock stone, bake them with vegetables. Eat with seasonings.

91. 龙虾冻 Lobster Jelly

制作者 黄健 张雄林

原料 Ingredient

龙虾 Lobster

凝胶粉 Jelly Powder

酸奶 Yogurt

水果丁 Diced Fruits

白葡萄酒 White Wine

盐 Salt

胡椒 Pepper

制作 Proceed

(1) 龙虾蒸熟，取出肉切片，用盐、胡椒和白葡萄酒腌渍入味。

Shell the steamed lobser. Shave the meat and marinate it with salt, pepper and white wine.

(2) 凝胶粉化开，上火烧开后冷却成□喱水。

Make jelly water.

(3) 虾片放入模具，小心倒入 喱水，放进冰箱冻定型后倒入盘中，盘边裱上酸奶，撒上水果丁即可。

Put the sliced lobster and jelly water into mould. Freeze it and take it out. Serve with yogurt and diced fruits.

92. 地中海石斑鱼 Mediterranean Sea Grouper

制作者 黄健 张雄林

原料 Ingredient

石斑鱼 Grouper
草虾 Shrimp
土豆泥 Mashed Potatoes
各式蔬菜丝 Sliced Vegetables
百里香 Thyme
混合香料 Mixed Herbs
面粉 Flour
蒜末 Chopped Garlic
红胡椒粒 Red Pepper
焦糖 Caramel
白葡萄酒 White Wine
橄榄油 Olive Oil
柠檬汁 Lemon Juice
盐 Salt
胡椒 Pepper

制作 Proceed

(1) 石斑鱼开成3片，用盐、白葡萄酒、柠檬汁和百里香腌渍。

Cut the grouper to three pieces. Marinate it with salt, white wine, lemon juice and thyme.

(2) 鱼片拍上面粉，用橄榄油煎一下，然后放入烤箱烤熟。

Soak the grouper in flour. Panfry it with olive oil then put it into oven to be done.

(3) 蒜末炒香，加入红胡椒粒、白葡萄酒、焦糖和柠檬汁，浓缩成甜酸汁。

Saute the chopped garlic, add red pepper, white wine, caramel and lemon juice, inspissate it.

(4) 鱼肉装盘，配上土豆泥、混合香料和炒熟并调味的各式蔬菜丝，淋入甜酸汁，上面再放一只烤好的草虾即可。

Put the fish on plate, serve with mashed potatoes, sliced vegetables, mixed herbs. Pour the sauce and garnish with baked shrimp.

93. 香酱扇贝王 Roasted King Scollop

制作者 黄健 张雄林

原料 Ingredient

扇贝王 King Scollop
青椒碎 Chopped Green Pepper
蛋白末 Chopped Egg White
番茄 Tomato
各式蔬菜 Vegetables
刁草 Dill
甜橙 Orange
番茄沙司 Tomato Sauce
奶油汁 Cream Sauce
白葡萄酒 White Wine
盐 Salt
胡椒 Pepper

制作 Proceed

(1) 扇贝王□水后用干净的口布吸干水分，批成两片。

Boil king scallop and cut it into two pieces.

(2) 将青椒碎和蛋白末用奶油汁、番茄沙司拌和待用。

Use the cream sauce and tomato sauce to marinate chopped green pepper, egg white and sliced tomato.

(3) 番茄切片，每一只扇贝王壳上放一片番茄片，再放上批成片的扇贝肉，浇上(2)中调制的酱，放进烤箱烤5分钟，取出装盘。

Slice the tomato, put it onto all scallop shell with scallop meat on it. Pour the cream sauce and tomato sauce. Put it in the oven to be finished.

(4) 各式蔬菜炒熟并调味，装入甜橙内作配菜，并以刁草点缀。

Serve with sauted vegetables, garnish with dill.

94. 挪威三文鱼 Grilled Salmon in Norwegian Style

制作者 黄健 张雄林

原料 Ingredient

三文鱼 Salmon
土豆 Potato
芦笋 Asparagus
胡萝卜 Carrot
柠檬片 Sliced Lemon
阿里根奴 Oregano
各式蔬菜丝 Sliced Vegetables
藏红花汁 Saffron Sauce
橄榄油 Olive Oil
盐 Salt
胡椒 Pepper

制作 Proceed

(1) 三文鱼用盐、胡椒、白葡萄酒、柠檬片和阿里根奴腌渍片刻。

Marinate salmon with salt, pepper, white wine, sliced lemon and oregano.

(2) 三文鱼用橄榄油煎一下，进烤箱烤至全熟。

Panfry salmon with olive oil to be medium and roast it to be done.

(3) 三文鱼装盘，配以炒熟并调味的各式蔬菜丝、土豆及芦笋等，淋上藏红花汁(注意泡开藏红花不要放水过多)即可。

Put the salmon on plate, serve with the sliced vegetables, potatoes and asparagus. Pour the saffron sauce.

95. 小龙虾汤 Baby Lobster Stock

原料 Ingredient

小龙虾 Baby Lobster
什菜 Mixed Vegetables
蒜末 Chopped Garlic
百里香 Thyme
刁草 Dill
洋葱 Onion
面粉 Flour
黄油 Butter
奶油 Cream
鱼汤 Fish Stock
白葡萄酒 White Wine
盐 Salt
胡椒 Pepper

制作 Proceed

(1) 龙虾拆取头、壳，放入烤箱烤香。

Use the head and shell of lobster, put them into oven to be done.

(2) 洋葱末与面粉用黄油炒香，加入改刀成块的什菜及蒜末，略炒。

Saute the chopped onion and flour with butter, mixed vegetables and chopped garlic.

(3) 加入龙虾头、壳和百里香、刁草、鱼汤，倒入白葡萄酒，烧开，再用小火煨烧，最后过滤出汤水。

Add the head and shell of lobster, thyme, dill, fish stock and white wine. Boil it then strain it.

(4) 将汤水浓缩至稠，加入奶油、少许白葡萄酒及盐、胡椒调味，装盘后以煮熟的龙虾肉和刁草装饰。

Inspissate the stock, add cream, white wine, salt and pepper. Put the stock in plate, garnish with boiled lobster meat and dill.

制作者 黄健 张雄林

96. 意大利烩海鲜 Stewed Seafoods in Italian Style

制作者 黄健 张雄林

原料 Ingredient

明虾 King Prawn
蛤蜊 Clam
黑鱼 Snakehead
三文鱼 Salmon
裙边 Lamboys
茄汁饭 Tomato Sauce Rice
胡萝卜 Carrot
芦笋 Asparagus
洋葱末 Chopped Onion
奶油 Cream
白葡萄酒 White Wine
盐 Salt
胡椒 Pepper

制作 Proceed

(1) 明虾等河海鲜取肉,□水后用黄油炒香。

Boil the seafoods then saute them with butter.

(2) 洋葱末炒香,投入海鲜等,加入白葡萄酒,浓缩一下,再加入奶油一起烩。

Put the chopped onion, seafoods, white wine. Inspissate it and stew it with cream.

(3) 调味后装入挖好的胡萝卜内,配上做熟的茄汁饭和芦笋。

Season it and put it into carrot, garnish with tamato sauce rice and asparagus.

97. 夏威夷蟹 Hawaii Crab

制作者 黄健 张雄林

原料 Ingredient

青蟹 Crab
小南瓜 Small Pumpkin
紫生菜丝 Sliced Red Lettuce
土豆泥 Mashed Potatoes
各式蔬菜粒 Diced Vegetables
蟹黄膏 Crab Meat
香菜叶 Coriander Leaves
混合香料 Mixed Herbs
洋葱末 Chopped Onion
白葡萄酒 White Wine
奶油 Cream
薄荷酱 Mint Paste
盐 Salt
胡椒粉 Pepper

制作 Proceed

(1) 青蟹蒸熟、拆肉，用混合香料、盐、胡椒和白葡萄酒腌渍入味。

Steam crab, use the meat. Marinate it with mixed herbs, salt, pepper and white wine.

(2) 蟹肉与土豆泥混合，做成蟹饼，放进烤箱烤至呈金黄色。

Mix the mashed potatoes and crab meat to make crab cake. Then put it into oven to be done.

(3) 洋葱末炒香，加白葡萄酒、薄荷酱和奶油，打匀并调味，即成薄荷沙司。

Saute the chopped onion, add white wine, mint paste, cream and seasoning.

(4) 蟹饼上浇上蟹黄膏，粘上香菜叶，再放进烤箱烤至上色，装盘，配上小南瓜、紫生菜丝和炒熟的各式蔬菜粒，淋入薄荷沙司即可。

Sprinkle crab meat and coriander leaves on the cake, put the cake into oven to be done, garnish with small pumpkin, sliced red lettuce and boiled vegetables. Pour the Mint sauce.

98. 新西兰牛排配明虾 Newzealand Tenderloin with King Prawn

制作者 黄健 张雄林

原料 Ingredient

牛排 Beef Tenderloin
明虾 King Prawn
米饭 Fragrant Rice
薯条 Potato Chips
芦笋 Asparagus
胡萝卜 Carrot
柠檬汁 Lemon Juice
咖喱粉 Curry Powder
洋葱末 Chopped Onion
羊肚菌汁 Morel Sauce
奶油白酒汁 Cream of White Wine Sauce
黄油 Butter
盐 Salt
胡椒 Pepper

制作 Proceed

(1) 牛排用盐、胡椒腌渍入味;明虾用柠檬汁腌渍片刻。

Marinate beef tenderloin with salt and pepper. Marinate king prawn with lemon juice.

(2) 米饭用咖喱粉和洋葱末炒成咖喱炒饭,再用模具成型,放入盘中。

Fry the rice with curry powder and chopped onion then put it in mould. Take it out and put it on plate.

(3) 牛排煎至五分熟,放在饭上,边上淋入羊肚菌汁(羊肚菌用波特酒浸泡)。

Panfry the beef tenderloin to medium well. Put it on the rice, pour the morel sauce around it.

(4) 明虾煎熟配在牛排旁,边上浇上奶油白酒汁,配上用黄油炒熟的芦笋等蔬菜及炸黄的薯条等即可。

Panfry king prawn to be done and put it beside the beef tenderloin, serve with sauted vegetables, potato chips, etc. Pour the cream of white wine sauce.

99. 香草羊排 Lamb Chop with Herbs

制作者 黄健 张雄林

原料 Ingredient

羊排 Lamb Chop
各式蔬菜 Vegetables
玉米片 Corns
百里香 Thyme
阿里根奴 Oregano
蒜头 Garlic
红菜头 Beet Root
干葱末 Chopped Shallot
芥末 Mustard
黄油 Butter
黄汁 Brown Sauce
白葡萄酒 White Wine
酸奶 Yogurt
盐 Salt
胡椒 Pepper

制作 Proceed

(1) 羊排用芥末、盐、胡椒、干葱末、白葡萄酒、百里香和阿里根奴腌渍。

Marinate the lamb chop with mustard, salt, pepper, chopped shallot, white wine, thyme and oregano.

(2) 各式蔬菜□水,用黄油炒熟,调味后装盘。

Blanch the vegetables and saute with butter and seasoning. Put them on plate.

(3) 干葱末炒香,加入黄汁,浓缩后调味。

Saute chopped shallot, add brown sauce. Inspissate it and season it.

(4) 羊排扒熟,放在蔬菜上,淋入干葱汁,以玉米片、酸奶、蒜头、红菜头等装饰。

Grill the lamb chop. Put it on the vegetables. Pour shallot sauce, garnish with corns, yogurt, garlic, beet root, etc.

100. 煎鹿肉配红酒汁 Panfried Venison with Red Wine Sauce

制作者 黄健 张雄林

原料 Ingredient

鹿肉 Venison
各式蔬菜 Vegetables
洋葱末 Chopped Onion
土豆片 Sliced Potato
百里香 Thyme
野味果 Juniper Berry
黄油 Butter
酸奶 Yogurt
红葡萄酒 Red Wine
红酒汁 Red Wine Sauce
盐 Salt
胡椒 Pepper

制作 Proceed

(1) 鹿肉切成厚片,加洋葱末、野味果、红葡萄酒、盐和胡椒腌渍后煎熟。

Slice the venison. Marinate it with chopped onion, juniper berry, red wine, salt and pepper and panfry it to be done.

(2) 各式蔬菜□水,用黄油加洋葱末炒熟,调味。

Blanch the vegetables, then saute them with chopped onion and seasoning.

(3) 鹿肉装盘,配以各式蔬菜,裱上酸奶,以炸土豆片及百里香装饰, 淋入红酒汁 (注意须用干红制作)。

Put the venison on plate, serve with vegetables and yogurt, garnish with sliced potatoes and thyme. Pour the red wine sauce.

101. 扒鳕鱼配甜椒汁 Grilled Codfish with Paprike Sauce

制作者 沈豪军

原料 Ingredient

鳕鱼 Codfish
各式蔬菜丝 Sliced Vegetables
红椒粉 Paprika
蒜末 Chopped Garlic
洋葱末 Chopped Onion
刁草 Dill
橄榄 Olive
黄汁 Brown Sauce
红葡萄酒 Red Wine
白兰地酒 Brandy
黄油 Butter
盐 Salt
胡椒 Pepper

制作 Proceed

(1) 鳕鱼去骨切中段，用盐、胡椒和白兰地酒腌渍，再放在扒炉上扒熟。

Grilled codfish marinated with salt, pepper and brandy.

(2) 将洋葱末、蒜末炒香，放入红椒粉、红葡萄酒、黄汁，浓缩，调味即成甜椒汁。

Fry the chopped onion and garlic then put red wine and brown sauce to inspissation. After seasoning, the paprika sauce is done.

(3) 将各式蔬菜丝用黄油炒熟，调味。

Saute sliced vegetables with butter and season.

(4) 将鱼装盘，甜椒汁淋在鱼身上，配以各式蔬菜丝，以刁草、橄榄点缀即可。

Put the codfish on plate. Pour the paprika sauce on the codfish and decorate plate with sliced vegetables, dill and olive to be done.

102. 扒三文鱼排配黑椒汁 Grilled Salmon with Black Pepper Sauce

制作者 沈豪军

原料 Ingredient

三文鱼 Salmon
土豆 Potato
各式蔬菜 Vegetables
洋葱末 Chopped Onion
蒜末 Chopped Garlic
黑胡椒碎 Crushed Black Pepper
红葡萄酒 Red Wine
白兰地酒 Brandy
牛奶 Milk
黄汁 Brown Sauce
黄油 Butter
盐 Salt
胡椒 Pepper

制作 Proceed

(1) 三文鱼用盐、胡椒、白兰地酒腌渍,再放在扒炉上扒熟。

Grill salmon marinated with salt, pepper and brandy, then let it be done.

(2) 将洋葱末、蒜末炒香,放入黑胡椒碎稍炒,加入红葡萄酒、黄汁,浓缩并调味,即成黑胡椒汁。

Saute chopped onion and garlic then add crushed black pepper, pour the red wine and brown sauce on it to finish the sauce.

(3) 将各式蔬菜用黄油炒熟,调味。

Saute vegetables with butter and season.

(4) 将土豆煮熟,碾成泥,放入烧开的牛奶,加盐、胡椒,调成土豆泥。

Boil potato and make it to mash mixed with boiled milk, salt and pepper.

(5) 三文鱼装盘,将黑胡椒汁淋在扒熟的鱼身上,配以各式蔬菜和土豆泥即可。

Put the salmon on plate, pour the black pepper sauce on, decorate plate with cooked vegetables and potato mash.

103. 焗文蛤 Baked Clam

制作者 沈豪军

原料 Ingredient

文蛤 Clam
青红椒粒 Chopped Green-red Capsicum
蘑菇片 Sliced Mushroom
荷兰芹末 Chopped Parsley
洋葱末 Chopped Onion
蒜头 Garlic
混合香料 Mixed Herbs
白兰地酒 Brandy
柠檬汁 Lemon Juice
黄油 Butter
盐 Salt
胡椒 Pepper

制作 Proceed

(1) 文蛤用开水稍烫，取出剥开。

Boil the clam. Get rid of carapace.

(2) 将洋葱末、蒜头、青红椒粒、蘑菇片、荷兰芹末与黄油、盐、胡椒、白兰地酒、柠檬汁混合均匀，放在文蛤肉上。

Mix the chopped onion, green-red capsicum, parsley, sliced mushroom, pepper, salt, butter, brandy and lemon juice. Then pour it on the clam.

(3) 将文蛤 焗熟，以混合香料等装饰即成。

Bake the clam to be done and decorate plate.

104. 烤林鱼红酒汁 Baked Lingfish with Red Wine Sauce

制作者 沈豪军

原料 Ingredient

林鱼 Lingfish
意大利节瓜 Zucchini
小胡萝卜 Baby Carrot
面包糠 Bread Crumbs
洋葱末 Onion
蒜末 Chopped Garlic
混合香料 Mixed Herbs
刁草 Dill
柠檬汁 Lemon Juice
白兰地酒 Brandy
红酒汁 Red Wine Sauce
黄油 Butter
盐 Salt
胡椒 Pepper

制作 Proceed

(1) 林鱼去骨切成块,用盐、胡椒、柠檬汁和白兰地酒腌渍,再放在扒炉上扒上色。

Chop the lingfish into pieces, marinate and grill it.

(2) 将面包糠、洋葱末、蒜末、混合香料、黄油混合,抹在鱼块上。

Put the bread crumbs, butter, mixed herbs, chopped onion, garlic on fish.

(3) 将鱼放入烤箱烤熟至呈金黄色,装盘,淋上红酒汁(做法参见第99页)即可。

Roast the fish to be done and put it on plate, then pour the red wine sauce on fish.

(4) 意大利节瓜调味后煎熟,小胡萝卜煮熟后调味,装盘作为配菜,以刁草点缀。

Panfry seasoned zucchini , boil baby carrots and season. Put them on plate, decorate with dill.

105. 烟熏三文鱼芝士卷 Smoked Salmon Camembert Filo Pastry

制作者 沈豪军

原料 Ingredient

烟熏三文鱼 Smoked Salmon
卡玛白特芝士 Camembert Cheese
面皮 Filo Pastry
鸡蛋 Egg
芒果肉 Mango Pulp
蛇果 Delicious
小番茄 Cherry Tomato
混合香料 Mixed Herbs
芒果汁 Mango Juice

制作 Proceed

(1) 将烟熏三文鱼和芝士用面皮包好卷起,面皮上刷少许蛋液。

Wrap the smoked salmon and camembert cheese with filo pastry. Place the cheese roll in smoked salmon & fillo pasery.

(2) 将三文鱼卷放进烤箱,烤至面皮呈金黄色取出。

Put it into oven to golden.

(3) 三文鱼卷装盘,淋上芒果汁,以芒果肉、蛇果、小番茄、混合香料装饰即可。

Put it on plate, serve with mango juice, mango pulp, delicious, cherry tomato and mixed herbs.

106. 酥香大虾 Baked King Prawn with Bread Crumbs Herbs

制作者 沈豪军

原料 Ingredient

明虾 King Prawn
芥末 Mustard
荷兰芹末 Chopped Parsley
新鲜百里香 Fresh Thyme
洋葱末 Chopped Onion
蒜末 Chopped Garlic
西芹 Celery
柠檬 Lemon
刁草 Dill
面包糠 Bread Crumbs
白兰地酒 Brandy
黄油 Butter
盐 Salt
胡椒 Pepper

制作 Proceed

(1) 将明虾后背切开。

Cut king prawn on backside.

(2) 将芥末、百里香、洋葱末、荷兰芹末、蒜末、盐、胡椒、黄油、面包糠及白兰地酒混合均匀，抹在虾背上。

Saute the prawn with mustard, thyme, chopped onion, parsley, garlic, salt, pepper, butter, bread crumbs and brandy.

(3) 将明虾放进烤箱烤熟，取出装盘，以西芹、柠檬及刁草装饰即可。

Put it into oven to be done. Then put it on plate, serve with celery, lemon and dill.

107. 烤牛柳配蘑菇汁 Roasted Beef Tenderloin with Mushroom Sauce

制作者 沈豪军

原料 Ingredient

牛柳 Beef Tenderloin
蘑菇片 Sliced Mushroom
洋葱末 Chopped Onion
小番茄 Cherry Tomato
意大利节瓜 Zucchini
土豆泥 Potato Mash
蒜末 Chopped Garlic
黄汁 Brown Sauce
红葡萄酒 Red Wine
黄油 Butter
盐 Salt
胡椒 Pepper

制作 Proceed

(1) 整条牛柳用盐、胡椒腌渍，稍煎后进烤箱，烤至半熟，取出切片装盘。

Marinate beef tenderloin with salt and pepper. Fry it for a little time then put into oven to be medium well. Cut it into pieces and decorate plate.

(2) 洋葱末、蒜末炒香，加入蘑菇片一起炒，再加入红葡萄酒、黄汁，浓缩、调味。

Saute chopped onion and garlic, blend with sliced mushroom. Then put red wine and brown sauce in. Inspissate and season it.

(3) 将蘑菇汁淋在牛柳上，配上土豆泥以及调味后煎熟的意大利节瓜，并以小番茄等装饰。

Pour the mushroom sauce on beef tenderloin to be done, serve with potato mash and zucchini, garnish with cherry tomatoes.

108. 什锦烧烤串 Mixed BBQ Skewer

制作者 沈豪军

原料 Ingredient

鲜贝 Scallop
大虾 Prawn
牛肉 Beef
鸡肉 Chicken
青红椒 Green-red Capsicum
洋葱 Onion
橄榄 Olive
BBQ 汁 BBQ Sauce
盐 Salt
胡椒 Pepper

制作 Proceed

(1) 鲜贝、大虾、牛肉、鸡肉用盐、胡椒腌渍入味,与青红椒、洋葱、橄榄一起用钢针串起扒熟。

Saute the scallop, prawn, beef, chicken to well. Skewer and grill them with green-red capsicum, onion and olive.

(2) 装盘,跟 BBQ 汁即可。

Put it on plate, serve with BBQ sauce.

109. 兔胸卷 Rabbit Breast Roll

制作者 沈豪军

原料 Ingredient

兔胸肉 Rabbit Breast
方腿 Ham
摩苏里拉芝士 Mozzarella Cheese
紫椰菜 Purple Broccoli
生菜 Lettuce
小胡萝卜 Baby Carrot
鸡蛋 Egg
面粉 Flour
面包糠 Bread Crumbs
白葡萄酒 White Wine
油醋汁 Vinaigrette Dressing
盐 Salt
胡椒 Pepper

制作 Proceed

(1) 兔胸肉用白葡萄酒、盐、胡椒腌渍，拍成片状，放入方腿、芝士，包成卷，拍上面粉，挂上蛋液，滚上面包糠，用温火炸熟。

Marinate the rabbit breast with white wine, salt and pepper. Beat it and wrap ham and cheese in. Soak into egg yolk and bread crumbs then panfry it.

(2) 兔肉卷改刀装盘，用生菜、紫椰菜、小胡萝卜(煮熟)装饰，淋入油醋汁即可。

Put the rabbit roll on plate, garnish with lettuce, purple broccoli and baby carrot, pour vinaigrette dressing.

110. 扒羊排配香草汁 Grilled Lamb Chop with Herb Sauce

制作者 沈豪军

原料 Ingredient

羊排 Lamb Chop
各式蔬菜 Vegetables
土豆饼 Potato Cake
迷迭香 Rosemary
刁草 Dill
洋葱末 Onion
蒜末 Garlic
黄汁 Brown Sauce
红葡萄酒 Red Wine
白兰地酒 Brandy
黄油 Butter
盐 Salt
胡椒 Pepper

制作 Proceed

(1) 羊排用盐、胡椒、迷迭香、红葡萄酒腌渍后扒熟。

Marinate lamb chop with salt, pepper, rosemary and red wine. Grill it to be done.

(2) 将洋葱末、蒜末炒香,加入迷迭香、红葡萄酒、白兰地酒、黄汁,调味、浓缩,即成香草汁。

Saute the chopped onion and garlic then mix with rosemary, red wine, brandy, brown sauce. Inspissate and season it.

(3) 将土豆饼煎熟垫入盘底,将羊排装盘,淋入香草汁,配以用黄油炒熟的各式蔬菜,以刁草装饰即可。

Fry potato cake and set to plate with lamb chop on. Pour the herb sauce on lamb chop. Serve with vegetables sauted with butter. Decorate the plate with dill.

111. 罗鲱鱼柳夹 Stuffing Herring Fish

制作者 邵军

原料 Ingredient

罗鲱鱼柳 Herring Fish
节瓜丝 Zucchini
茄子丝 Eggplant
番茄汁 Tomato Sauce
柠檬汁 Lemon Juice

制作 Proceed

(1) 罗鲱鱼用盐、胡椒、白酒、柠檬汁腌渍约 10 分钟。

Marinate herring fish with salt, pepper, white spirit and lemon juice for 10 minutes.

(2) 将鱼柳放入煎盘，用中火煎熟至色嫩黄。

Panfry the fish.

(3)将鱼柳装盆，配上蔬菜，淋入烧热的番茄汁。

Put the panfried fish on the plate,serve with vegetables and tomato sauce.

112. 厚烤豆腐 Baked Tofu

原料 Ingredient

绢豆腐 Silk Tofu
木鱼汤 Wooden Fish Soup
淡口酱油 Soy Sauce
味淋 Mirin
木鱼花 Wooden Fish Flower

制作 Proceed

(1) 将出水的豆腐以高油温炸至呈金黄色，再放在火炉上烤至两面呈深褐色，装盆。

Deep-fry the silk tofu to golden, then bake the both sides of it to brown.

(2) 木鱼汤加淡口酱油、味淋、清酒、海鲜素及少量盐，烧开，淋于豆腐上，撒上木鱼花和京葱丝。

Add the soy sauce, mirin, sake, seafood su into wooden fish soup and bring to boil. Pour the soap on the tofu, sprinkled with wooden fish flower and Beijing onion.

制作者 邵军

113. 烤茄子 Roasted Eggplant

制作者 邵军

原料 Ingredient

茄子 Eggplant
木鱼花 Wooden Fish Flower
生姜泥 Mashed Ginger
黄瓜 Cucumber
木鱼汤 Wooden Fish Soup
浓口酱油 Soy Sauce
味淋 Mirin
清酒 Sake
海鲜素 Seafood Su

制作 Proceed

(1) 将新鲜茄子放在炭火上烤至皮呈深褐色，取出，以最快的速度剥去皮。

Roast the fresh eggplant to brown, then peel it.

(2) 把茄子肉切成段，装盆，撒上木鱼花，配以生姜泥和黄瓜。

Cut the eggplant into sections, sprinkled with wooden fish flower, served with the mashed ginger and the cucumber.

(3) 木鱼汤加浓口酱油、味淋、清酒及海鲜素，烧开，作为跟汁。

Add the soy sauce, mirin, sake, seafood su into wooden fish soup and bring to boil, as with the Juice.

114. 煎羊排配薄荷酒汁 Fried Lamb Chop Sauced with Creme De Menthe

制作者 邵军

原料 Ingredient

羊排 Lamb Chop
薄荷酒 Creme de Menthe
蟹肉 Crab meat
米饭 Rice
脆饼 Crackers
酸奶 Yogurt
番茄汁 Tomato Juice
蒜茸 Garlic
姜汁 Ginger Juice

制作 Proceed

(1) 羊排用薄荷酒及香料腌制。

Marinate the Lamb chop with spices and creme de menthe.

(2) 将米加入蟹肉、蒜茸、姜汁、番茄汁煨熟。

Add crab meat, garlic, ginger, tomato juice into rice, then cook them well.

(3) 将煎熟的羊排和米饭装盆，淋上酸奶和薄荷酒汁。

Arrange the grilled lamb chop and rice on a plate, topped with yogurt sauce and Creme De Menthe.

115. 生渍珍雕鱼片 Marinated Snapper

制作者 邵军

原料 Ingredient

珍雕鱼(鲷鱼) Snapper
橄榄油 Olive Oil
刁草 Dill
生菜 Lettuce
胡萝卜丝 Shredded Carrot
洋葱丝 Shredded Onion
柠檬汁 Lemon Juice
盐 Salt
胡椒 Pepper

制作 Proceed

(1) 珍雕鱼取肉去皮，用盐、胡椒、柠檬汁、刁草和橄榄油腌渍。

Use the meat of snapper, marinate it with salt, pepper, lemon juice, dill and olive oil.

(2) 胡萝卜丝、洋葱丝等用盐、胡椒、柠檬汁腌渍。

Marinate shredded carrot, onion, etc. with lemon juice, salt and pepper.

(3) 盘内放上生菜，将腌好的鱼肉批成薄片摆放在生菜上，用胡萝卜丝、洋葱丝等装饰即可。

Put the lettuce on plate. Slice the marinated snapper and put it on the lettuce, garnish with shredded carrot, onion, etc.

116. 双味摩司塔 Two-flavor Mousse Tower

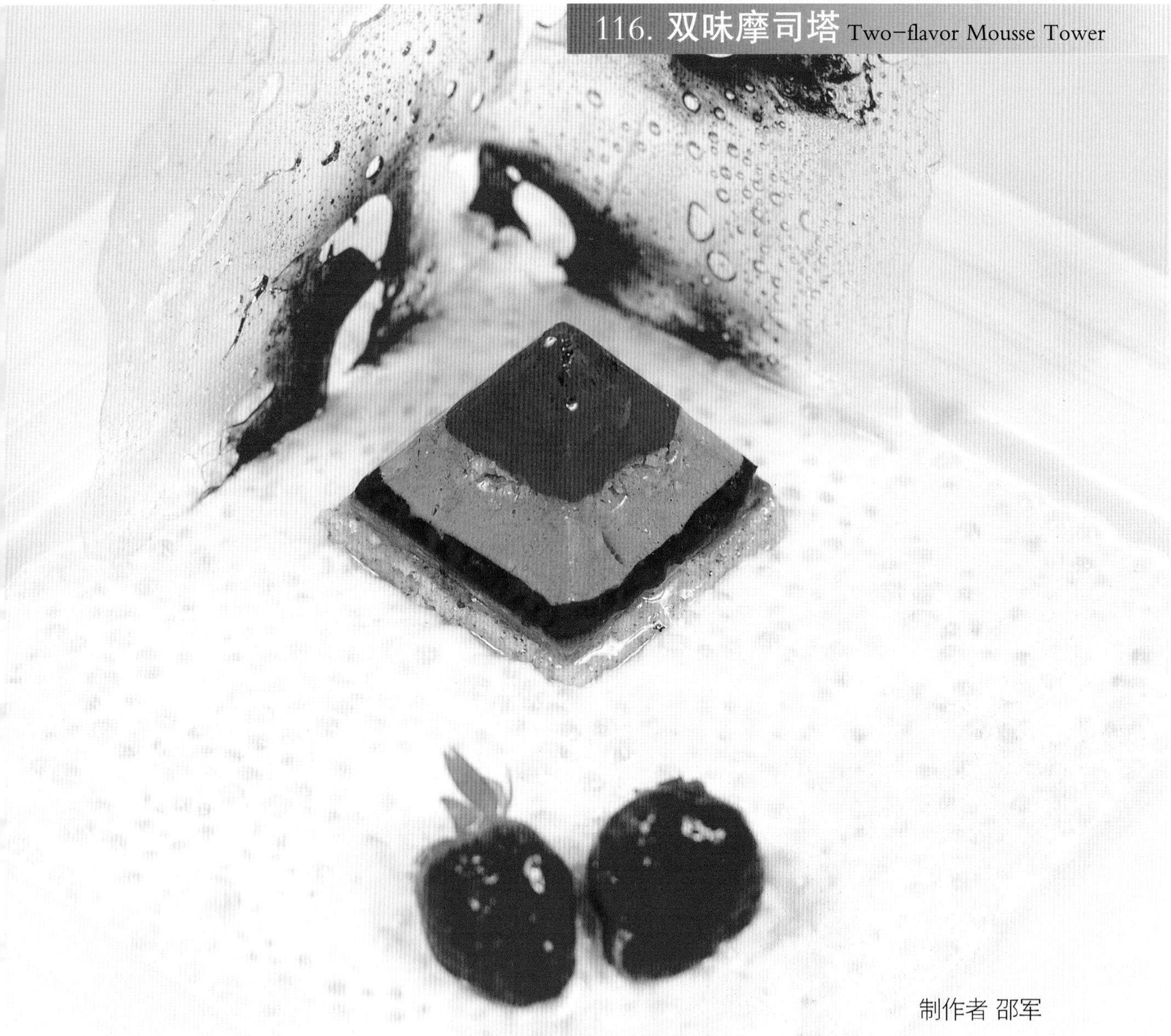

制作者 邵军

原料 Ingredient

巧克力摩司 Chocolate Mousse
可可摩司 Cocoa Mousse
冰淇淋 Ice cream
千层酥皮 Puff Pastry
糖片 Sugar
草莓 Strawberry

制作 Proceed

(1) 将巧克力慕斯和可可慕斯调匀后倒入模具内，放入冰箱冷冻。

Mix the chocolate mousse and cocoa mousse, then frozen it in the mold.

(2) 将千层酥皮与冰淇淋放在盘中央，上面扣上慕斯。

Put puff pastry and ice-cream on a plate, topped with the mousse.

(3) 加上糖片与草莓装盘。

Serve with sugar and strawberry.

117. 煎鹅肝配羊肚菌汁 Grilled Goose Liver with Morel Sauce

制作者 邵军

原料 Ingredient

鹅肝 Goose Liver
各式蔬菜 Vegetables
羊肚菌 Morel
蘑菇 Mushroom
混合香料 Mixed Herbs
洋葱末 Chopped Onion
白兰地酒 Brandy
黄汁 Brown Sauce
红葡萄酒 Red Wine
盐 Salt
胡椒 Pepper

制作 Proceed

(1) 鹅肝切成厚片，放入混合香料、盐、胡椒和白兰地酒腌渍片刻。

Cut the goose liver to pieces then marinate it with mixed herbs, salt, pepper and brandy.

(2) 用煎盘将鹅肝煎熟。

Grill the goose liver to be done.

(3) 将羊肚菌和洋葱末炒香，加入红葡萄酒，浓缩一下，加入黄汁，调味后即成羊肚菌汁。

Saute the morels and chopped onion, add red wine and inspissate it. Add brown sauce and seasoning.

(4) 装盘时用炒好的蔬菜和蘑菇垫在盘中，鹅肝放在上面，淋上羊肚菌汁即可。

Put goose liver on plate, garnish with fried vegetables and mushrooms, pour morel sauce.

118. 煎牛柳 Panfried Beef Tenderloin

制作者 邵军

原料 Ingredient

牛柳 Beef Tenderloin
各式蔬菜 Vegetables
土豆 Potato
雪梨酒汁 Shirley Wine Sauce
盐 Salt
黑胡椒 Black Pepper
洋葱末 Chopped Onion
草莓 Strawberry

制作 Proceed

(1) 牛柳用盐、黑胡椒、洋葱末腌渍一下。

Marinate the beef tenderloin with salt, pepper, black pepper and chopped onion.

(2) 牛柳煎至所需的成熟度。

Grill the beef tenderloin.

(3) 装盘时将炒好的各式蔬菜垫在牛柳下面，配上炸黄的土豆，淋上雪梨酒汁(其上可放土豆球)，以草莓点缀即可。

Garnish with fried vegetables, potato, shirley wine sauce, etc.

119. 兔肉卷 Rabbit Roll

制作者 邵军

原料 Ingredient

兔胸 Rabbit Breast
兔腿 Rabbit Leg
各式蔬菜 Vegetables
混合香料 Mixed Herbs
焦糖 Caramel
黑醋 Balsamico Vinegar
洋葱末 Chopped Onion
红葡萄酒 Red Wine
盐 Salt
胡椒 Pepper
葱 Shallot

制作 Proceed

(1) 兔胸用盐、胡椒和混合香料腌渍,然后将炒过的各式蔬菜放入,卷起,用保鲜膜包裹,放入开水中煮熟。

Marinate the rabbit breast with salt and pepper, roll it up by fried vegetables ,wrapped with plastic film then boiled to be done.

(2) 兔腿用混合香料、盐、胡椒和红葡萄酒腌渍并烤熟。

Marinate the rabbit leg with mixed herbs, salt, pepper and red wine then fry it.

(3) 将洋葱末炒香,加混合香料、红葡萄酒和黑醋,浓缩,加盐、胡椒及焦糖调味,即成焦糖黑醋汁。

Saute the chopped onion, add mixed herbs, red wine, balsamico vinegar. Inspissate it, add salt, pepper and caramel.

(4) 兔胸、兔腿装盘,淋上焦糖黑醋汁,以葱装饰。

Put all ingredients on plate, pour the sauce(3), decorated to be finish.

120. 小牛肉鹅肝配白兰地鹅肝汁 Roasted Veal and Goose Liver with Brandy Goose Liver Sauce

制作者 邵军

原料 Ingredient

小牛肉 Veal
鹅肝 Goose Liver
各式蔬菜 Vegetables
蘑菇 Mushroom
番茄 Tomato
洋葱末 Chopped Onion
白兰地酒 Brandy
红葡萄酒 Red Wine
黄汁 Brown Sauce
牛奶 Milk
黄油 Butter
盐 Salt
胡椒 Pepper

制作 Proceed

(1) 将小牛肉用盐、胡椒、红葡萄酒腌渍;鹅肝改刀后浸入牛奶中。

Marinate the veal with salt, pepper and red wine. Immerse the goose liver in milk.

(2) 分别将小牛肉和鹅肝煎熟装入盘中。

Roast the veal and goose liver to be done.

(3) 另取鹅肝,加洋葱末口炒,加入少许白兰地酒以及黄汁,烧开后打碎,浓缩并调味,再淋上白兰地酒。

Saute another goose liver with chopped onion, add brown sauce and a little brandy. Boil and blend it then inspissate and season. Pour brandy again.

(4) 各式蔬菜与蘑菇用黄油炒熟并调味,装盘做装饰,淋上白兰地鹅肝汁即可。

Serve with fried vegetables and mushrooms. Pour the brandy goose liver sauce.

121. 煎小明虾色拉 Grilled Prawn Salad

制作者 郑纯涛

原料 Ingredient

小明虾 Small Prawn
面包片 Sliced Bread
混合生菜 Mixed lettuce
樱桃番茄 Cherry Tomato
柠檬汁 Lemon juice
白酒 White Spirit
油醋汁 Oil vinegar
盐 Salt
胡椒 Pepper

制作 Proceed

(1) 小明虾去头、壳,留尾,用柠檬汁、白酒、盐、胡椒腌渍。

Peel the small prawn with tail left, marinated with lemon juice, white spirit, salt and pepper.

(2) 取煎盘将腌好的小明虾煎熟。

Pan-fry the marinated small prawn.

(3) 将面包片烘至呈金黄色。

Bake sliced bread to golden.

(4) 装盆时,面包片垫在明虾下面,用生菜、樱桃番茄等装饰,淋入油醋汁。

Arrange the sop on a plate, topped with small prawn, garnished with lettuce and cherry tomato, sprinkled with oil vinegar.

122. 三文鱼太太 Salmon Tartar

制作者 郑纯涛

原料 Ingredient

新鲜三文鱼肉 Fresh Salmon
红菜头(熟)Beetroot(cooked)
水瓜柳 Capers
黑鱼子 Black Caviar
番茄粒 Tomato Cubes
橙肉 Orange Flesh
芫荽末Chopped Parsley
柠檬汁Lemon Juice
酸奶Yogurt
辣根Horseradish
油醋汁Oil Vinegar

制作 Proceed

(1) 三文鱼肉、红菜头分别切成细粒,用柠檬汁、辣根、盐腌渍 10 分钟左右,放入洋葱末、水瓜柳和芫荽末拌匀。

Marinate the minced salmon and beetroot for 10 minutes, fold in lemon juice, chopped onion, capers and chopped parsley.

(2) 将红菜头粒挤干水分后放入模具中,压紧,上面再放入鱼肉粒,压紧。

Drain minced beetroot. Put it into mold, topped with minced salmon, then compress.

(3) 轻轻地将模具脱出,鱼肉上面裱上酸奶,放少许黑鱼子,淋上油醋汁。盆边撒上番茄粒、橙肉、芫荽末即可。

Take the mold out. Mount yogurt on the salmon, topped with black caviar, sprinkled with oil vinegar, garnished with tomato cubes, orange flesh and chopped parsley.

123. 香焗蓝口贝 Baked Blue Mussel

制作者 郑纯涛

原料 Ingredient

青口贝 Blue Mussel
卷心菜 Cabbage
番茄 Tomato
罗勒叶 Basil leaves
橄榄油 Olive oil
盐 Salt
胡椒 Pepper
小茴香籽 Cumin

制作 Proceed

(1) 青口贝放入开水中烫至贝壳张开，卷心菜切丝，罗勒叶切丝，番茄切成粒。

Cook the blue mussel to be well done. Cut cabbage and basil leaves into slices. Cut tomato into tablets.

(2) 番茄粒、罗勒叶丝加入橄榄油、盐、胡椒，拌匀后浇在贝肉上。

Mix and fold the tomato tablets, cabbage slices, olive oil, salt and pepper. Pour them on the blue mussel.

(3) 将青口贝放入□炉内□熟。

Bake the blue mussel.

(4) 将卷心菜丝、番茄粒、罗勒叶丝和青口贝一同装盆。

Arrange the cabbage slices, tomato tablets, basil leave slices with blue mussel on a plate.

124. 海鲜包配沙巴翁 Seafood Roll Served with Sabayon

制作者 郑纯涛

原料 Ingredient

虾仁 Shelled Shrimp
鳟鱼肉 Trout Fish
鲜贝 Scallop
目鱼 Cuttle Fish
青口贝 Blue Mussel
洋葱末 Chopped Onion
奶油 Cream
白酒 White Spirit
薄面饼 Thin Bread
鸡蛋 Egg
黄油 Butter

制作 Proceed

(1) 用黄油先将洋葱末炒香,投入虾仁等海鲜粒,翻炒,再加入白酒,稍作浓缩后加入奶油和盐、胡椒调味,待奶油汁浓缩至稠,盛出放在薄面饼中。

Saute seafood tablets with chopped onion, white spirit, cream, salt and pepper. Then boil it to dense as sauce. Soon after pour the sauce on thin bread.

(2) 蛋黄加入白酒、盐、胡椒,隔水加热并打泡,即成沙巴翁。

Add white spirit, salt, pepper into egg yolk. Then heat and whip it to foam as sabayon.

(3) 将薄面饼折叠包起后放在盆内,淋上沙巴翁即可。

Fold the thin bread, sprinkled with sabayon.

125. 帕尔玛火腿煎小牛肉 Parma Ham with Veal

制作者 郑纯涛

原料 Ingredient

小牛肉 Veal

帕尔玛火腿 Parma Ham

各式蔬菜 Assorted Vegetables

草莓 Strawberry

面粉 Flour

野米饭 Wild Rice

鼠尾草 Sage

雪梨酒 Sherry

黄汁 Brown Sauce

黄油 Butter

制作 Proceed

(1) 小牛肉用盐、胡椒、鼠尾草、白酒腌渍入味。

Marinate the veal with salt, pepper, sage, white spirit seasoning.

(2) 帕尔玛火腿刨成薄片,贴在小牛肉上,沾上面粉,放入煎盘中煎至所需的成熟度。

Stick sliced Parma ham on veal, coated with flour. Pan-fry the veal to be well done.

(3) 黄汁中加入雪梨酒,浓缩后加盐、胡椒调味。

Pour Sherry into the brown sauce. Boil it to dense, add salt and pepper seasoning.

(4) 煎好的小牛肉装盆,配以各式蔬菜和野米饭,将(3)淋在牛肉旁,以草莓作装饰即可。

Arrange the fried veal on a plate, served with assorted vegetables and wild rice. Sprinkle (3) at the veal aside, garnished with strawberry.

126. 帕尔玛火腿卷肉眼 Parma Ham Roll Stuffed Rib Eye

制作者 郑纯涛

原料 Ingredient

牛肉眼 rib eye

帕尔玛火腿 Parma Ham

各式蔬菜 Assorted Vegetables

土豆 Potato

洋葱末 Chopped Onion

红胡椒粒 Red Pepper Sauce

黄汁 Brown Sauce

黄油 Butter

橄榄油 Olive Oil

红酒 Red Wine

制作 Proceed

(1) 牛肉眼用橄榄油、盐、胡椒、红酒腌渍，包上帕尔玛火腿薄片煎烤至熟。

Marinate the rib eye with olive oil, salt, pepper and red wine. Then wrap the Parma ham to pan-fry.

(2) 用黄油将洋葱末炒香，加红胡椒粒、红酒，浓缩后再倒入黄汁，加盐调味即成红胡椒粒汁。

Saute chopped onion with butter, add red pepper and red wine. Boil it to dense, add brown sauce, salt as red pepper sauce.

(3) 装盆，配以各式蔬菜和土豆，淋上红胡椒粒汁即可。

Arrange the ham roll on a plate,served with assorted vegetables and potato, sprinkled with red pepper sauce.

127. 鹅肝烤羊排 Roasted Lamb Chop with Goose Liver

制作者 郑纯涛

原料 Ingredient

羊排 Lamb Chop
鹅肝 Goose Liver
蘑菇 Mushrooms
各式蔬菜(节瓜、圆椒等) Vegetables
红鱼子 Red Caviar
迷迭香 Rosemary
红葡萄酒 Red Wine
黑菌汁 Truffle Sauce
黄油 Butter
盐 Salt
胡椒 Pepper

制作 Proceed

(1) 将羊排用盐、胡椒和红葡萄酒腌渍入味;鹅肝煮熟、调味,碾成酱;蘑菇切片。

Marinate the lamb chop with salt, pepper and red wine. Mash the boiled goose liver. Slice the mushrooms.

(2) 羊排煎上色,涂上鹅肝酱,蘑菇一片片整齐地排放在鹅肝酱上,将羊排包住,放入烤箱内烤至七分熟。

Grill the lamb chop. Put some mashed goose liver and sliced mushrooms. Put it in the oven to medium well.

(3) 各式蔬菜口水,用黄油炒熟并调味。

Saute the vegetables blanched with butter and seasoning.

(4) 羊排改刀置于盘中,配上蔬菜,淋上黑菌汁(做法参见第10页),以红鱼子及迷迭香点缀即可。

Put the lamb chop on the plate, serve with vegetables and truffle sauce. Garnish with red caviar and rosemary.

128. 煎牛柳配野菌汁 Grilled Filet with Mushroom Sauce

制作者 郑纯涛

原料 Ingredient

牛柳 Beef Filet
红椰菜 Red Cabbage
面包球 Bread Ball
野菌 Wild Mushrooms
百里香 Thyme
洋葱末 Onion
红酒 Red Wine
黄汁 Brown Sauce
黄油 Butter

制作 Proceed

(1) 牛柳加盐、胡椒、百里香、红酒腌渍入味，煎至所需的成熟度。

Marinate the filet with salt, pepper, thyme and red wine. Pan-fry it to be well done.

(2) 用黄油将洋葱末炒香，加入野菌、红酒、黄汁、盐、胡椒，烧开，收浓。

Saute the chopped onion with butter, add wild mushrooms, red wine, brown sauce, salt and pepper. Then boil it to dense.

(3) 煎好的牛柳装入盆内，配上红椰菜和面包球。

Arrange the filet on a plate, served with red cabbage and bread ball.

129. 香草羊排配干葱汁 Grilled Lamb Chops with Shallot Sauce

制作者 郑纯涛

原料 Ingredient

羊排 Lamb chops
土豆 Potato
胡萝卜 Carrot
节瓜 Zucchini
干葱末 Dry Spring Onion
芥末 Mustard
阿里根奴 Oregano
百里香 Thyme
白酒 White spirit
黄油 Butter

制作 Proceed

(1) 羊排用芥末、盐、胡椒、干葱末、白酒、百里香、阿里根奴腌渍入味。

Marinate the lamb chops with mustard, salt, dry spring onion, white spirit, thyme and oregano.

(2) 土豆、胡萝卜、节瓜改刀成形,分别口水后用黄油煎炒成熟,加盐、胡椒调味。

Slice the potatoes, carrots and zucchinis. Saute the blanched pieces with butter, add salt and pepper.

(3) 干葱末炒香,加入黄汁,收浓后加盐、胡椒调味,即成干葱汁。

Saute the dry spring onion, add brown sauce. Boil it with salt and pepper as dry spring onion sauce.

(4) 将羊排放在扒炉上扒至所需的成熟度,取出搁放在盆内,配上土豆、胡萝卜、节瓜,淋入干葱汁即可。

Grill the lamb chops. Arrange the cooked chops on a plate, served with potatoes, carrots and zucchinis, sprinkled with dry spring onion sauce.

130. 榛子冰淇淋摩丝球 Hazelnut Ice-Cream Mousse Ball

制作者 郑纯涛

原料 Ingredient

榛子 Hazelnut

冰淇淋 Ice-cream

巧克力丝 Shredded Chocolate

车厘子酱 Blackberry Paste

金酒 Dry Gin

制作 Proceed

(1) 将调好的摩丝与冰淇淋、榛子拌匀,冷冻后制成球形并加入巧克力。

Mix mousse, ice-cream and hazelnut, then refrigerate it into a ball, and add chocolate.

(2) 把巧克力丝、车厘子酱与摩丝冰淇淋一同装盆。

Arrange the shredded chocolate, blackberry paste and ice-cream ball on a plate.

131. 焗鸡胸配姜味浓缩汁 Baked Chicken Breast Served with Ginger Juice

制作者 凌

原料 Ingredient

鸡胸 Chicken Breast
各色甜椒 Assorted Bell Pepper
各色生菜 Assorted Greens
鲜西柚汁 Fresh Grapefruit Juice
脆炸甜姜丝 Deep-fried Candied Ginger
碎香茅 Chopped Lemongrass
冰花梅酱 Plum Sauce
碎剁椒 Chopped Hot Chili
生姜汁 Ginger Juice
姜汁酒 Ginger Wine
美洲中度辣椒粉 Cayenne Pepper

制作 Proceed

(1) 用香茅、冰花梅酱、碎剁椒和干葱腌制鸡胸并放入冰箱保存 3 个小时。

Marinate the chicken breast with lemongrass, plum sauce, chopped hot chili and shallot, place it in cooler for 3 hours.

(2) 将甜椒切条并在西柚汁里面煨熟，将鸡胸从冰箱内取出放入烤箱在 180 摄氏度下烤制 12 分钟至熟。

Cut the sweet pepper into strips and boil with grapefruit juice, bake the chicken at 180℃ for 12 minutes until cooked.

(3) 装盆，将酱汁淋于鸡胸肉上，用少许生菜和脆生姜丝装饰即可。

Place the glazed peppers across the center of plate, and put the sliced chicken breast on top, drizzle the sauce on the plate, and garnish with mixed greens and crispy ginger.

132. 烤芦笋配帕尔马火腿 Roasted Asparagus Served with Parma Ham

制作者 凌云

原料 Ingredient

嫩芦笋段 Asparagus
牛油果肉 Avocado
熟鸡蛋 Boiled Egg
帕尔马火腿 Parma Ham
新鲜西洋 Fresh Watercress Leaves
新鲜紫苏 Fresh Basil
橄榄油 Olive Oil
奶油风味香草沙拉酱 Creamy Herb Dressing
盐和胡椒 Salt and Pepper

制作 Proceed

(1) 烤芦笋至熟备用。

Grill the asparagus with olive oil until cooked.

(2) 将所有原材料装盆并淋上奶油风味香草沙拉酱，用新鲜紫苏叶装饰。

Arrange all ingredients on a plate and top with creamy herb dressing, garnish with fresh basil leave.

133. 西西里风味明虾色拉 Sicilian-style Prawn Salad

制作者 凌云

原料 Ingredient

大明虾 King Prawn

比利时苈苣

Belgian Endive

熟莲藕片

Cooked Lotus

青豆角

Blanched Green Beans

青橄榄

Stuffed Green Olives

柠檬汁 Lemon Juice

意大利沙拉汁

Golden Italian Dressing

盐和胡椒

Salt and Pepper

制作 Proceed

(1) 将明虾去壳用盐和胡椒腌制片刻,在油锅中煎至嫩熟。

Peel the prawn, season with salt and pepper, and pan-fry it until cooked.

(2) 混合所有的蔬菜,并洒上碎欧芹。

Mix all vegetables, sprinkled with chopped parsley.

(3) 在蔬菜上摆好明虾,淋上意大利沙拉汁。

Place the prawn on the vegetables, add golden Italian dressing.

134. 马沙拉烤羊排 Masala Crusted Lamb Chops

制作者 凌云

原料 Ingredient

羊排 Lamb Chops
红腰豆 Red kidney Beans
芦笋头 Asparagus Tips
金黄脆蒜片 Deep-fried Sliced Garlic
印度孜然辣酱 Indian Masala Stir-fry Seasoning
豆豉 Black Beans
陈皮末 Air-dried Orange Peel
新鲜橙皮 Fresh Orange Peel
黄汁 Brown Sauce
无盐黄油 2 汤匙 Unsalted Butter

制作 Proceed

(1) 羊排用印度孜然辣酱腌制，煎烤待用。

Marinate the lamb chops with masala seasoning, panfry and bake it until cooked.

(2) 热油锅，炒制蒜泥和豆豉 1 分钟，喷红酒，加入调匀的黄汁，加入新鲜橙皮继续加热 10 分钟。

Saute garlic mud and black bean for 1 minute, sprinkled with red wine and pour into brown sauce. Add the orange peel to cook 10 minutes.

(3) 将所有原料装盆，淋少许汁酱，用新鲜迷迭香装饰即可。

Arrange all the ingredients on a plate, top with sauce, and garnish with fresh rosemary.

135. 椒香烤牛柳 Grilled Fillet Mignon with Pepper

制作者 凌云

原料 Ingredient

牛柳子 Beef Fillet Mignon
去壳新鲜蚕豆 Fresh Broad Beans
鲜百里香叶 Fresh Thyme
巴蜀风味麻辣腌料 Sichuan Spicy Marinade
各式混合胡椒粒 Mixed Peppercorn
红葡萄酒 Red Wine
碎葱 Chopped Shallot
黄汁 Brown Sauce
盐和胡椒 Salt and Pepper

制作 Proceed

(1) 牛排用巴蜀风味腌料腌制 30 分钟，然后两面煎至金黄并烤至五分熟。

Marinate the beef in Sichuan Spicy Marinade for 30 minutes. Grill the beef until mine rare.

(2) 蚕豆过水后，加入葱花用橄榄油清炒，并用盐和胡椒调味。

Blanch the broad beans and stir-fry with chopped shallot, season with salt and pepper.

(3) 菜肴装盘后淋上汁水，并装点少许百里香。

Arrange all the ingredients on a plate, top with sauce, and garnish with fresh thyme.

136. 煎石斑柳配夏多内葡萄酒汁 Grilled Grouper Fillet with Chardonnay

制作者 凌云

原料 Ingredient

石斑鱼柳 Grouper Filler
土豆 Potato
青节瓜 Zucchini
樱桃番茄 Cherry Tomato
肉豆蔻粉 Nutmeg Powder
意大利黑醋 Balsamic Vinegar
鸡蛋清 Egg White
夏多内白葡萄酒 Chardonnay
白汁 White Sauce

制作 Proceed

(1) 将将石斑鱼柳用盐和胡椒腌制片刻,煎熟待用。

Marinate the grouper filler in salt and pepper for minutes, then panfry the fish.

(2) 土豆切细丝加入肉豆蔻粉和栗粉,混拌均匀,煎成薄饼,煎 4 分钟至其呈金黄色。

Mix the julienne potato with nutmeg and cornstarch to make a rosti .Pan-fry it for about 4 minutes until crispy.

(3) 将打发的蛋清缓缓倒入白汁均匀搅拌,将鱼柳装盘,并淋汁,用葱段点缀。

Whisk the egg white until stiff and stir it slowly into white sauce. Arrange the fish on a plate, top with sauce, garnish with chive.

137. 三文鱼排配青芥汁 Salmon Fllet with Creamy Wasabi Sauce

制作者 凌云

原料 Ingredient

三文鱼排 Salmon Fillet
意粉 Pasta
各式蔬菜丝 Assorted Sliced Vegetables
青橄榄 Green Olive
京葱丝 Shredded Beijing Onion
新鲜莳萝草 Fresh Dill Grass
白葡萄酒 White Wine
柠檬汁 Lemon Juice
青芥汁 Wasabi Sauce
白汁 White Sauce

制作 Proceed

(1) 用开水加白酒和柠檬汁烫熟三文鱼排。

Poach the fish fillet in water with wine and lemon juice until cooked.

(2) 然后将青芥末慢慢细致地打匀入白汁。

Stir the wasabi into the white sauce.

(3) 将三文鱼排放置在意粉上方,配上青橄榄。

Place the fish filet on top of pasta and garnish with green olive.

138. 煎龙虾仔配松露汁 Seared Lobster with Truffle

制作者 凌云

原料 Ingredient

新鲜扇贝 Fresh Scallop
龙虾仔 Baby Lobster Shelled
菠菜意大利饺 Spinach Ravioli
薄脆片 Crisps
碎干葱 Chopped Shallot
马德拉酒 Madeira Wine
松露油 Truffle Oil
白汁 White Sauce
新鲜奶油 Fresh Cream

制作 Proceed

(1) 用盐和胡椒腌制海鲜片刻,煮熟菠菜意大利饺。

Marinate the seafood in salt and pepper for minutes, boil the spinach ravioli.

(2) 将松露菌和酒倒入过滤好的白汁,收汁至质地醇滑。

Pour the truffle oil and wine into the white sauce, cook it until sauce dries up with smooth.

(3) 把海鲜煎熟,喷白酒,与意大利饺装盆,并用薄脆片和萝卜苗装饰。

Panfry the seafood, sprinkled with wine. Arrange them with ravioli on a plate, garnish with crisps and chervil.

139. 奶油蘑菇汤配鹅肝酱吐司 Cream of Mushroom Soup with Foie Gras Crostini

制作者 凌云

原料 Ingredient

野米 Wild Rice
意大利米 Arborio Rice
橄榄油 Olive Oil
蒜泥 Minced Garlic
碎欧芹 Chopped Parsley
巴马臣芝士碎 Parmesan Cheese Grated
面包脆 Crostini
鹅肝慕斯 Foie Gras Mousse
蘑菇 Mushroom
新鲜奶油 Fresh Cream

制作 Proceed

(1) 蘑菇口炒,加入汤水并搅碎。

Saute the mushrooms, add soup and minced.

(2) 野米和意大利米煮熟调味。

Put wild rice and Arborio rice in the water boiled to be done.

(3) 将鹅肝慕斯均匀涂抹于面包脆表面。

Smear the Foie Gras on the crostini.

(4) 蘑菇汤撒上碎欧芹,和鹅肝吐司、面包脆、野米饭一起装盆。

Garnish the soup with chopped parsley, and serve with Foie Gras,wild rice and crostini.

140. 蒸鳕鱼配芦笋 Steamed Codfish Served with Asparagus

制作者 凌云

原料 Ingredient

鳕鱼 Codfish
橄榄酱 Olive Sauce
黑橄榄 Black Olive
洋葱碎 Chopped Onion
橄榄油 Olive oil
酸豆 Anchovy
土豆泥 Mashed Potatoes
红甜椒 Red Pepper
嫩芦笋 Asparagus
莳萝 Dill

制作 Proceed

(1) 在蒸烤炉中将腌制好的鳕鱼蒸熟。
Steam the salted codfish in steam oven.

(2) 把橄榄酱等配料搅拌后,淋放在蒸熟的鳕鱼上。
Stir the olive sauce with the other seasonings, pour it on top of steamed cod.

(3) 在盘中先淋红椒汁,再放土豆泥,将鳕鱼置于土豆泥上,配芦笋和莳萝做装饰。
Sprinkle the red pepper sauce on a plate, cover the mashed potatoes, top with codfish, then garnish with asparagus and dill.

141. 各式小吃 Assorted Appetizer

制作者 马光俊

原料 Ingredient

烤鳗 Grilled Eel
牛油果 Avocado
金枪鱼 Tuna Fish
黄瓜 Cucumber
腌制三文鱼 Marinated Salmon
蟹仔 Crab Roe
米饭 Rice
虾仁 Shelled Shrimp
柠檬 Lemon

制作 Proceed

(1) 将烤鳗、熟虾仁及牛油果、米饭做成寿司。

Make sushi from grilled eel, shelled shrimp, avocado and rice.

(2) 黄瓜装入蟹仔，三文鱼用橄榄油及柠檬腌制，金枪鱼裹上椒盐轻煎，一同装盘即可。

Fill the crab roes into the cucumber. Marinate the salmon with olive oil and lemon. Wrap the tuna with spiced salt ,then panfry.Arrange them on a plate.

142. 波士顿龙虾薄荷酸奶汁 Poached Boston Lobster with Mint Yogurt

制作者 马光俊

原料 Ingredient

波士顿龙虾 Boston Lobster
酸奶 Yogurt
薄荷叶 Mint Leave
黄瓜 Cucumber
芦生菜 Arugula
橙 Orange
草莓 Strawberry

制作 Proceed

(1) 将龙虾过水煮熟，把龙虾肉取出待用。
Blanch the lobster, take its meat out.

(2) 黄瓜切成薄片摆出造型，与龙虾肉和芝麻菜装盘。
Arrange the lobster meat and the arugula on a plate, served with sliced cucumber.

(3) 用橙肉和薄荷酸奶汁及橙皮丝装饰。
Garnish the food with orange segments, mint yogurt and orange peel.

143. 轻煎金枪鱼色拉 Seared Tuna Fish Salad

制作者 马光俊

原料 Ingredient

金枪鱼 Tuna Fish
生菜 Lettuce
鸽蛋 Pigeon egg
樱桃番茄 Cherry Tomato
香葱 Chive
比利时生菜 Endive

制作 Proceed

(1) 将金枪鱼裹上调味和黑胡椒煎至表面香脆。

Wrap the tuna pieces with black pepper and seasoning ,then panfry them to be done.

(2) 用鸽蛋做成荷包蛋备用。

Fry the pigeon eggs.

(3) 将混合生菜和金枪鱼及鸽蛋装盆, 用香葱及樱桃番茄装饰。

Arrange the mixed lettuce, tuna and pigeon eggs on the plate, garnish with chive and cherry tomato.

144. 奶油鲜笋汤配脆腌肉 Creamy Asparagus Soup with Crisp Bacon

制作者 马光俊

原料 Ingredient

芦笋 Asparagus

酸奶油 Sour Cream

莳萝 Dill

腌肉 Bacon

奶油 Cream

制作 Proceed

(1) 鲜芦笋加水煮烂,打成汁放入奶油调味。

Boil the asparagus to mush. Then beat it into juice, add cream in seasoning.

(2) 将汤装盆后用鲜芦笋、腌肉、莳萝和酸奶油装饰。

Pour the soup into tureen, garnish with fresh asparagus, dill and sour cream.

145. 蟹仔意大利面 Crab Roe Spaghetti

制作者 马光俊

原料 Ingredient

意大利面 Spaghetti
蟹仔 Crab Roe
蛋黄酱 mayonaise 50g
小葱 spring onion10g
紫菜丝 sea weed 5g
柴鱼片 katsuobushi

制作 Proceed

(1) 意大利面用开水煮 12 分钟。
Boil the spaghetti for 12 minutes.

(2) 将蟹仔和蛋黄酱拌匀备用。
Mix the sauce with crab roe and mayonnaise.

(3) 用橄榄油将意大利面炒一下调味,用调好的酱拌匀装盘。
Sauté the spaghetti with olive oil to fry about seasoning, folded in the sauce.

(4) 放入小葱、紫菜丝、柴鱼片和蟹仔装饰。
Garnish the spring onion, sea weed, katsuobushi and crab roes.

146. 煮海鲜配藏红花汁 Stew Seafood Served with Saffron

制作者 马光俊

原料 Ingredient

大虾 Prawn
青口贝 Blue Mussel
澳带 Scallop
蛤蜊 Clam
广式馄饨 Cantonese Wonton
三文鱼籽 Salmon Roe
藏红花 Saffron
奶油 Cream
紫苏 Basil

制作 Proceed

(1) 将大虾、澳带及青口贝煮熟待用。

Boil the prawns, scallops and blue mussels to be done.

(2) 广式馄饨过水煮熟。

Cook Cantonese wontons.

(3) 将海鲜和馄饨装盆，淋上藏红花汁沙司。用三文鱼籽及紫苏装饰即可。

Put the wontons and seafood on a plate, topped with saffron sauce, garnish with salmon roe and basil.

147. 扒海鲜红椒汁 Grilled Seafood with Red Pepper Sauce

制作者 马光俊

原料 Ingredient

澳带 Scallop

香茅 Lemon grass

小八爪鱼 Baby Squid

银鳕鱼 Codfish

生菜 Lettuce

红椒汁 Red Pepper

血柚 Pink Grapefruit

制作 Proceed

(1) 扒银鳕鱼、香茅澳带串及小八爪鱼至熟。

Grill the codfish, the baby squids ,and the brochette with lemongrass and scallop.

(2) 用新鲜的红椒做成沙司备用。

Make sauce with fresh red pepper sauce.

(3) 将海鲜装盘,用生菜和血柚装饰。

Arrange all the seafood on a plate, garnish lettuce and pink grapefruit.

148. 海鲜串配椰汁香菜饭 Seafood Yakitori with Coconuts Milk Rice

制作者 马光俊

原料 Ingredient

虾仁 Shelled shrimp
澳带 Scallop
银鳕鱼 Cod
青口贝 Mussel
米饭 Rice
芒果沙沙 Mango Salsa
香茅 Lemon grass
椰汁 Coconut Milk

制作 Proceed

(1) 用香茅将青口贝、澳带、虾仁及银鳕鱼串烤。

String the blue mussel s, scallops and shelled shrimps with lemongrass as Yakitori.

(2) 将芒果切丁放入橄榄油,调味备用。

Dice the mango, seasoning with olive oil.

(3) 用椰汁和香菜将白米饭拌匀装盘。

Fold coconut milk and coriander in white rice, then arrange the plate.

(4) 芒果沙沙装饰。

Garnish the food with mango salsa.

149. 烟熏鸭胸配时蔬 Smoked Duck Breast with Seasonal Vegetable

制作者 马光俊

原料 Ingredient

鸭胸 Duck Breast
鸡腿菇 Coprinus
香菇 Black Mushroom
豌豆 Pea
豆瓣 Braad Bean
红皮萝卜 Radish

制作 Proceed

(1) 将鸭胸用椒盐、茶叶和香料烟熏。
Smoke the duck breast with spiced salt, tea and flavoring.

(2) 将时蔬□水。
Blanch the vegetables.

(3) 将切开的鸭胸和时蔬装盆。
Arrange the dissected duck breast and vegetables on a plate.

150. 炭烤牛柳配意大利黑醋汁 b.b.q Tenderloin Served with Balsamic Cream

制作者 马光俊

原料 Ingredient

牛里脊 Tenderloin

帕玛火腿 Parma Ham

芦笋 Asparagus

樱桃番茄 Cherry Tomato

马苏里拉芝士 Mozzarella Cheese

黑醋汁 Balsamic Cream

豆瓣 Brord Bean

阿里根奴 Oregano

制作 Proceed

(1) 牛柳炭烤至五分熟。

Char-grilled the tenderloin to mine rare.

(2) 将牛柳切开摆放,架上芦笋、火腿、番茄及马苏里拉芝士串。

Chop up the tenderloin, topped with asparagus, ham, tomato and mozzarella string cheese.

(3) 淋上黑醋汁,用豆瓣装饰。

Sprinkle balsamic cream on the food, garnished with bean.

151. 海鲜开拿批 Seafood Canapé

制作者 莫自杰

原料 Ingredient

澳带 Scallop

草虾 Shrimp

烟熏三文鱼 Smoked Salmon

油浸金枪鱼 Canned Tuna in Oil

吐司面包 Toast Bread

蛋黄酱 Mayonnaise

混合生菜 Mixed lettuce

制作 Proceed

(1) 将澳带煎熟，切成小丁，用蛋黄酱拌合，金枪鱼也用蛋黄酱拌合，草虾□熟后剥去头、壳。

Dice the fried Scallops, mix with mayonnaise and canned tuna。Shuck the blanched shrimp.

(2) 生菜刻成面包片相仿的块，放在面包片上，然后将草虾仁和烟熏三文鱼分别用牙签插在面包片上固定，将澳带和金枪鱼也分别放在面包片上。

Put the lettuces on the bread-chips, joined with grass shrimp and smoked salmon, topped with scallop and tuna.

(3) 将海鲜排放在盆中，用生菜装饰。

Arrange the seafood on a plate, garnished with lettuce.

152. 黄瓜慕斯 Cucumber Mousse

制作者 莫自杰

原料 Ingredient

黄瓜 Cucumber

□哩粉 Jelly powder

甜奶油 Sweet Cream

草莓 Strawberries

薄荷叶 Mint Leaves

制作 Proceed

(1) □喱粉用水化开，烧滚后自然冷却，加入甜奶油。

Pour cold water in the Jelly powder, boil it. After-cooling, add the sweet cream.

(2) 将黄瓜茸、黄瓜粒一同加入□喱水中，倒入模具，放入冰箱中冷冻成形。

Then put the minced cucumber in, refrigerate it in the mold.

(3) 将成形的□哩冻倒出模具，装入盆内，用草莓、薄荷叶装饰即可。

Arrange jelly on the plate, garnished with strawberries and mint leaves.

153. 海鲜拼盆 Seafood Plate

制作者 莫自杰

原料 Ingredient

三文鱼 Salmon
扇贝 Scallop
北极贝 North Pole Clam
珍珠蚌 Pearl Oyster
玉兰菜 Endive Lettuce
辣根 Houseradish
柠檬 Lemon
甜橙汁 Orange Juice
罗勒叶 Basil leaves
橄榄油 Olive Oil
盐 Salt

制作 Proceed

(1) 将三文鱼、扇贝用盐、胡椒和柠檬汁腌渍,北极贝和珍珠蚌改刀待用。

Marinate the salmon and scallop with salt, pepper and lemon juice. Slice the north pole clam and pearl oyster.

(2) 将三文鱼折成花朵状,扇贝煎至呈金黄色。

Make the salmon like flower. Gril the scallop.

(3) 甜橙汁加罗勒叶、柠檬肉及橄榄油,混合成柠檬罗勒甜橙汁。

Mix orange juice, basil leaves, lemon pulp and olive oil.

(4) 将三文鱼花放在盘中央,辣根垫在盘中分成三堆,分别放上扇贝等海鲜,插上玉兰菜,淋上柠檬罗勒甜橙汁。

Set the salmon to the center. Put the houseradish and seafoods around. Garnish with endive lettuce and lemon basil orange sauce.

154. 金枪鱼太太 Tuna Fish Salad

制作者 莫自杰

原料 Ingredient

金枪鱼 Tuna Fish
洋葱 Onion
荷兰芹末 Chopped Parsley
黄瓜 Cucumber
红菜头 Beet Root
红鱼子 Red Caviar
水果丁 Fruits Dice
柠檬汁 Lemon Juice
酸奶 Yogurt
盐 Salt
胡椒 Pepper

制作 Proceed

(1) 金枪鱼、洋葱、黄瓜分别切成粒，红菜头煮熟并调味后也切成粒。

Dice the tuna fish, onion and cucumber. Boil the beet root, season and cut it to grains.

(2) 将金枪鱼与洋葱粒、荷兰芹末混合，加盐、胡椒、柠檬汁拌匀。

Mix the tuna fish with chopped onion and parsley, add salt, pepper and lemon juice.

(3) 黄瓜粒用酸奶拌匀后放入模具内，压紧后再加入红菜头，再压紧，最后放入金枪鱼，取出模具装盘，以红鱼子及水果丁装饰即可。

Mix cucumber and yogurt and impact them into mould then put the chopped beet root on it. Lastly put tuna fish on. Take it out mould, decorate plate to be done.

155. 轻煎大明虾 Panfried King Prawn

制作者 莫自杰

原料 Ingredient

明虾 King Prawn
墨鱼汁 Cuttle Fish Sauce
混合香料 Mixed Herbs
百里香 Thyme
洋葱末 Chopped Onion
鱼汤 Fish Stock
黄油 Butter
柠檬汁 Lemon Juice
白葡萄酒 White Wine
盐 Salt
胡椒 Pepper

制作 Proceed

(1) 明虾用混合香料、盐、胡椒、柠檬汁和白葡萄酒腌渍 15 分钟,再用小火煎熟,装盘。

Marinate the king prawn with mixed herbs, salt, pepper, lemon juice and white wine for 15 minutes. Panfry king prawn to be done. Put it on plate.

(2) 洋葱末用黄油炒香,加白葡萄酒后浓缩,再加少许鱼汤及深海墨鱼汁,调味后淋入盘中,并以百里香装饰。

Saute chopped onion with butter, add white wine and inspissate the sauce. Then add fish stock and cuttle fish sauce. After seasoning, put it into plate. Garnish with endive lettuce and thyme.

156. 香煎味啉三文鱼 Fried Mirin Salmon

制作者 莫自杰

原料 Ingredient

米饭 Rice
味啉 Mirin
红菜头 Beetroot
三文鱼 Salmon
柠檬汁 Lemon Juice
白酒 White spirit
新鲜车厘子 Fresh Cherries
肉桂粉 Cinnamon
蜂蜜 Honey

制作 Proceed

(1) 三文鱼用米鳞腌制，虹彩豆用肉桂粉、蜂蜜腌制。

Marinate the salmon with mirin, and marinate the rainbow beans with cinnamon and honey.

(2) 将三文鱼煎至五分熟，红菜头煨熟。

Panfry the salmon to mine rare, Stew beetroot cooked.

(3) 将红菜头铺在盆中，放上熟三文鱼，淋上车厘子汁。

Cover the beetroot on a plate, topped with fried salmon, sprinkled with cherries juice.

157. 海鲜鳕螺配草莓汁 Cod snails with Strawberry Sauce

制作者 莫自杰

原料 Ingredient

金鳕螺肉 Cod Snails
澳带 Scallop
比利时蓝贝青口 Leon de Bruxelles
草莓块 Strawberry Pieces
草莓汁 Strawberry Juice
蕃茄汁 Tomato Juice
白酒 White spirit
洋葱末 Minced Onion
蒜泥 Minced Garlic
黄油 Butter
盐 Salt
胡椒 Pepper

制作 Proceed

(1) 将金鳕螺肉、澳带、蓝贝青口在开水中烫一下。
Blanch the cod snails, scallops, leon de bruxelles. Set aside.

(2) 澳带用盐、胡椒拌腌后放入煎盘中煎熟。
Marinate the scallops with salt, pepper, then panfry them.

(3) 另取锅加黄油,将蒜泥□香,加入蓝贝青口、白酒和番茄汁,煮至篮贝青口断生。
Saute the minced garlic with butter.Add the leon de bruxelles , white spirit and tomato juice, boil to well-done.

(4) 装盆时,将螺肉放在盆中央,旁边用澳带、蓝贝青口等围边,淋上汁水。
Arrange the cod snails on a plate, garnished with the scallops and the leon de bruxelles, sprinkled with sauce.

158. 煎银鳕鱼配黑醋酒汁 Fried Cod Served with Black Vinegar Sauce

制作者 莫自杰

原料 Ingredient

银鳕鱼 Cod Fish

柠檬 Lemon

芦笋 Asparagus

意大利面 Pasta

洋葱 Onion

蒜茸 Minced garlic

白兰地 Brandy

香料 Spices

制作 Proceed

(1) 银鳕鱼用柠檬、白兰地、香料、盐、胡椒腌制。

Marinate the cod fish with lemon, brandy, spices, salt and pepper.

(2) 用蒜茸、洋葱、香料等炒熟意大利面。

Saute the pasta with minced garlic, onion and spices.

(3) 煎熟银鳕鱼和意大利面装盆，淋上黑醋酒汁。

Arrange the fried cod fish and pasta on a plate, sprinkle with black vinegar.

159. 蔬菜酿海鲜 Roasted Vegetables and Seafoods

制作者 莫自杰

原料 Ingredient

各式海鲜 Seafoods

各式蔬菜(节瓜、胡萝卜等) Vegetables

黑菌 Truffle

百里香 Thyme

红葡萄酒 Red Wine

波特酒 Port Wine

日式酱汁 Japanese Soy Sauce

柠檬汁 Lemon Juice

白葡萄酒 White Wine

制作 Proceed

(1) 将各式海鲜打碎,加入柠檬汁、白葡萄酒、盐、胡椒、百里香和波特酒腌渍;各式蔬菜切成条状调味。

Mash the seafoods. Marinate with lemon juice, white wine, salt, pepper, thyme and port wine. Season julienne vegetables.

(2) 将蔬菜放入圆形模具内,中间塞入海鲜,用保鲜膜包住,放入烤箱隔水烤熟。

Make the stuffed seafoods then put it in the oven to do well.

(3) 取下模具,将烤好的料置入盘中,黑菌用红葡萄酒煨熟做装饰,淋上日式酱汁即可。

Put the seafoods on plate. Garnish with truffle boiled with red wine, and pour Japanese soy sauce.

160. 煎羊排配红酒汁 Fried Lamb Chops Served with Red Wine Sauce

制作者 莫自杰

原料 Ingredient

羊排 Lamb Chops
鹅肝 Goose Liver
各式蔬菜 Kinds of Vegetables
鹅肝酱 Foie Gras
牛奶 Milk
红酒 Wine
黄汁 Brown Sauce
百里香 Thyme
洋葱末 Chopped Onion
阿里根奴 Oregano
黄油 Butter
盐 Salt
胡椒 Pepper

制作 Proceed

(1) 羊排用红酒、百里香、阿里根奴、盐、胡椒腌制入味，鹅肝改刀成厚片，泡入牛奶和红酒的混合液中。

Marinate the lamb chops with wine, thyme, oregano ,salt and pepper. Slice the goose liver, immerse in a mixture of milk and wine.

(2) 将腌好的羊排煎至所需的成熟度，鹅肝取出，用黄油煎熟。

Fried the lamb chop. Fried the marinated foie gras cru with butter.

(3) 用黄油将洋葱末炒香，加入鹅肝酱、红酒、黄汁收浓后，加盐、胡椒调味，即成鹅肝红酒汁。

Saute the chopped onion with butter.Pour in the foie gras , wine, brown sauce, add salt and pepper to cook as sauce.

(4) 装盆时鹅肝覆盖在羊排上，配上各式蔬菜，淋入烧热的鹅肝红酒汁。

Cover the fried foie gras on the lamb chops, served with the fresh vegetables, sprinkled with hot foie gras red wine sauce.

161. 帕尔玛火腿蜜瓜香橙沙律 Parma Ham with Fresh Fruit

制作者 周剑伟

原料 Ingredient

帕尔玛火腿 Parma Ham

蜜瓜 Honey Melon

橙 Orange

罗勒 Basil

制作 Proceed

(1) 橙肉切片打底。

Slice the orange meat and put them on a plate.

(2) 蜜瓜肉改刀外卷帕尔玛火腿薄片。

Wrap the sliced honey melon with Parma ham.

(3) 装盆淋上醋汁,用橙片、罗勒点缀即可。

Sprinkle vinegar sauce on the fruit and ham, garnished with orange slices and basil.

162. 牛油果与大虾色拉 King Prawn Salad with Avocado

制作者 周剑伟

原料 Ingredient

明虾 King prawn

牛油果 Avocado

红心柚 Pink Grapefruit

意大利黑醋 Black Vinegar

制作 Proceed

(1) 明虾与杂菜、香料一起煮熟去壳留尾。

Boil the king prawn with vegetables and spices. Peel the prawn with tail left.

(2) 牛油果、红心柚取其肉并改刀。

Take the meat from avocado and pink grapefruit, then slice it.

(3) 装盆时淋上黑醋汁即可。

Arrange the food on a plate, sprinkled with black vinegar.

163. 青龙虾配鱼子酱 Lobster Served with Caviar

制作者 周剑伟

原料 Ingredient

小青龙虾 Lobster

鳄梨酱 Avocado Mousse

黑鱼子酱 Black Caviar

青瓜 Pickle

制作 Proceed

(1) 龙虾煮熟取肉切厚片待用。

Slice the cooked lobster fillet to take stand-by.

(2) 青瓜去皮□水调味。

Blanch the peeled pickle with seasoning.

(3) 红酒醋放少许糖浓缩至稠。

Boil the red wine vinegar with a little sugar to dense.

(4) 装盆配鳄梨酱,点上黑鱼子酱即可。

Arrange the food on a plate, served with avocado sauce and black caviar.

164. 香煎黑鲷鱼配芒果沙司 Pan-Fried Snapper Fillet with Mango Sauce

制作者 周剑伟

原料 Ingredient

黑鲷鱼 Black Snapper

芒果 Mango

黑豆 Black Bean

制作 Proceed

(1) 黑鲷鱼柳调味,卷成形,煎熟。

Pan-Fry the marinated black snapper fillet in roll forming.

(2) 芒果丁、熟黑豆、口茜碎、番茄丁调味拌橄榄油。

Mix the diced mango, black beans, tomatoes, parsley and seasoned with olive oil.

(3) 土豆泥、山药泥拌匀调味。

Mashed the potatoes, yams mud season.

(4) 装盆浇上沙司。

Put them on a plate with sauce.

165. 炭烤澳洲带子配鳄梨酱 Char-grilled Scallops Served with Avocado Mousse

制作者 周剑伟

原料 Ingredient

澳洲带子 Scallops
红鱼子酱 Red Caviar
鳄梨 Avocado Mousse
花菜 Cauliflower
土豆 Potato
豆苗 Pea Shoot
金针菜 Day Lily
杏仁 Almond

制作 Proceed

(1) 带子调味烤熟。
Grill the flavored scallops.

(2) 花菜、土豆、杏仁煮熟，调味，加工成茸状。
Cook and process the cauliflower, potatoes, almonds like velvet with seasoning.

(3) 豆苗、金针菜放入炸成形的馄饨皮中。
Put the pea shoot and day lily into deep-fried wonton skins.

(4) 装盆时放上红鱼子酱，淋上鳄梨酱。
Arrange the food on a plate, topped with red caviar, sprinkled with avocado mousse.

166. 巧克力蟹钳肉配咖啡沙司 Chocolate in Crab Meat with Coffee Sauce

制作者 周剑伟

原料 Ingredient

花蟹钳 Crab meat

白巧克力碎 White chocolate

浓缩咖啡 Concentrated coffee

西芹 Celery

制作 Proceed

(1) 花蟹钳蒸熟取其肉,放入香料和西芹末调味拌匀。

Take the meat from steamed crab claws, mixed with spices and chopped parsley.

(2) 将白巧克力与蟹肉制作成蟹钳的形态。

Make the white chocolate and crab meat into the shape of claw.

(3) 咖啡制作成沙司配其旁边装盆。

Arrange the crab meat and chocolate on a plate, served with coffee sauce.

167. 香煎银鳕鱼 Pan-Fried Cod Fish

制作者 周剑伟

原料 Ingredient

银鳕鱼 Cod fish

培根 Bacon

兰刀豆 Lentil Bean

蘑菇 Mushroom

番茄 Tomato

口茜 Parsley

制作 Proceed

(1) 银鳕鱼柳外包培根，煎熟色呈金黄。

Wrap the cod fillet with bacon, pan-fry to golden.

(2) 熟兰刀豆用洋葱、培根、蘑菇、番茄、口茜炒香加入番茄酱烩。

Saute the cooked lentil beans with onions, bacon, mushrooms, tomatoes, add tomato sauce.

(3) 装盆用杂生菜点缀。

Arrange the food on a plate, decorated with mixed lettuce.

168. 坚果牛肉卷配番茄汁 Nuts in Beef Roll with Tomato Juice

制作者 周剑伟

原料 Ingredient

牛肉 Beef
坚果 Nuts
金针菇 Golden Mushroom
番茄汁 Tomato Sauce
春卷皮 Spring Roll Wrapper
芦笋 Asparagus

制作 Proceed

(1) 薄牛肉片调味，外裹青葱、金针菇、碎坚果炸熟成卷待用。

Wrap the marinated beef slices with scallion, golden mushroom and chopped nuts, deep-fry to rolls.

(2) 春卷皮卷芦笋炸脆。

Roll the asparagus with spring roll wrapper, deep-fry them crispy.

(3) 将金针菇等蔬菜调味放入去籽番茄内。

Put the golden mushrooms and the other vegetables into the seedless tomatoes.

(4) 装盆时淋上番茄汁。

Arrange the plate, topped with tomato sauce.

169. 蓝莓乳酪蛋糕 Blueberry Cheese Cake Canapé

制作者 孙玉明

原料 Ingredient

奶油芝士 Cream Cheese

淡奶 Cream

细砂糖 Refined Sugar

鸡蛋 Eggs

蓝莓果馅 Blueberry Fruit Filling

饼干屑 Biscuits

黄油 Butter

制作 Proceed

(1) 蛋黄加入细砂糖打松。

Whisk the egg yolks with refined sugar.

(2) 加入软化好的奶油芝士。

Add the softened cream cheese.

(3) 加入打发至六成的淡奶。

Add the cream foaming to 60 per.

(4) 将模具放入冰箱冷冻即可。

Pour the Sauce into the mold to become formed in refrigerator.

170. 摩卡香蕉摩斯 Coffee Banana Mousse

制作者 孙玉明

原料 Ingredient

牛奶 Milk

鲜奶油 Fresh Cream

咖啡 Coffee

鸡蛋 Eggs

细砂糖 Refined Sugar

香蕉 Bananas

明胶 Gelatin

制作 Proceed

(1) 蛋黄加糖打松。

Whisk the egg yolks with sugar.

(2) 牛奶、鲜奶油打至六成,加入明胶。

Foam the cream to 60 per.Add milk and gelatin.

(3)将上述原料拌匀。

Mix the above ingredients.

(4) 将模具放入冰箱冷冻即可。

Pour the Sauce into the mold to become formed to refrigerator.

171. 日式芝麻鱼(冷菜) Tuna Carpaccio with White Radish Salads

制作者 李伟强 徐高治

原料 Ingredient

金枪鱼 Tuna Fish
白芝麻 White Sesame
黑芝麻 Black Sesame
生抽 Soya bean Sauce
青柠汁 Lime Juice
麻油 Sesame Oil
萝卜片 White Radish
蛋黄酱 Mayonnaise
芥末 Wasabi

制作 Proceed

(1) 将金枪鱼切成长条,放上芝麻煎炸上色。

Pan fry the tuna bars coated with sesame.

(2) 将生抽、青柠汁、麻油调匀后加入白萝卜片腌制一天左右。

Marinate the white radish slices with soy sauce, lemon juice, sesame oil for one day.

(3) 将蛋黄酱和芥末混合成酱汁。

Mix the mayonnaise and wasabi as sauce.

(4) 萝卜片铺在盆底,放上金枪鱼,淋上酱汁。

Cover the radish slices on a plate, topped with tuna bars, sprinkled with sauce.

172. 芒果澳带（冷菜）Marinated Scallop with Cucumber & Mango Salsa

制作者 李伟强 徐高治

原料 Ingredient

澳带 Scallop
芒果酱 Mango Salsa
小黄瓜 Small Cucumber
葱丝 Spring Onion
红椒丝 Shredded Red Pepper
橄榄油 Olive Oil
蒜头 Garlic
盐 Salt
胡椒粉 White Pepper

制作 Proceed

(1) 将澳带浸泡在摄氏 55 度左右的蒜香橄榄油里 5 分钟。

Marinate the scallop in garlic olive oil at 55℃ for 5 minutes.

(2) 黄瓜切薄片腌制。

Marinate the cucumber slices.

(3) 黄瓜片铺在盆底，上放澳带，淋上芒果酱。

Cover the cucumber slices on a plate, topped with scallop, sprinkled with mango salsa.

173. 奶油泡沫青豆鹅肝汤 Creamy Green Pea and Foie Gras Soup

制作者 李伟强 徐高治

原料 Ingredient

青豆 Green Pea

鸡汤 Chicken Soup

盐 Salt

胡椒粉 White Pepper

鹅肝 Goose Liver

培根碎 Chopped Bacon

牛奶 Milk

制作 Proceed

(1)青豆用鸡汤煮烂,打碎过滤取汁。

Boil the green pea to mush with chicken soup, whip and filter it to get sauce.

(2)鹅肝切小块煎熟。

Pan-fry goose liver slices.

(3) 青豆汁倒入杯中,淋上打发的牛奶,佐鹅肝块。

Pour the green bean sauce into a pot, sprinkled with foaming milk, served with the fried goose liver slices.

174. 南瓜汤配大虾 Pumpkin Soup with Pan-fried King Prawn

制作者 李伟强 徐高治

原料 Ingredient

大虾 King Prawn
老南瓜 Pumpkin
洋葱 Onion
牛奶 Milk
奶油 Cream
松仁 Pine Nuts
薄脆 Crispy
胡椒 Pepper
盐 Salt

制作 Proceed

(1) 老南瓜去皮去籽放入鸡汤煮烂。加入奶油打碎成汤。

Boil the peeled pumpkin to mush with chicken soup. Add cream in and whip it.

(2) 大虾腌制后煎熟。

Pan-fry the marinated prawn to be done.

(3) 将南瓜汤倒入杯中,洒上松仁,佐大虾、薄脆饼。

Pour the pumpkin soup into a pot, sprinkled pine nuts, served with crispy.

175. 煎大虾配蒜香奶油 Pan Fried King Prawns Served with Garlic Cream

制作者 李伟强 徐高治

原料 Ingredient

大虾 King Prawns
红尖椒 Red Chill
香茅 Lemongrass
洋葱 Onion
蒜香奶油 Garlic Cream Sauce
大蒜头 Garlic
大葱 Leek
淡奶油 Whipping Cream
盐 Salt
胡椒粉 White Pepper

制作 Proceed

(1) 将大虾开背去头去沙后洗干净加红椒、香茅、干葱、色拉油、盐、胡椒调味煎熟待用。

Pan fry the headless prawns with red peppers, lemongrass, dried onions, salad oil, salt and pepper.

(2) 将红椒、香茅、干葱、色拉油打碎后倒入淡奶油,收浓,过滤。

Grind the red peppers, lemongrass, dried onions and salad oil, add whipping cream, then boil and filter to get sauce.

(3) 大虾装盆,淋上汁水。

Arrange the prawns on a plate, sprinkled with sauce.

176. 日式香煎银鳕鱼 Pan-fried Cod Fish with Miso & Lemongrass Tomato Sauce

制作者 李伟强 徐高治

原料 Ingredient

银鳕鱼 Cod Fish

小青菜 Chinese Cabbage

番茄香茅汁 Lemongrass Tomato Sauce

茄子泥 Eggplant Mush

味曾酱 Miso

京葱丝 Shredded Beijing Onion

薄脆 Crispy

盐 Salt

胡椒粉 White Pepper

制作 Proceed

(1) 将银鳕鱼用味曾酱腌制煎上色后烤熟。

Grill the cod fish marinated with miso.

(2) 蔬菜炒熟,待用。

Saute the vegetables, stand-by.

(3) 将银鳕鱼装盆,配上蔬菜,淋上汁水。

Arrange the cod fish on a plate, served with vegetables, sprinkled with sauce.

177. 酒香芒果配冰激凌及沙巴翁汁 Wine Mango Served with Ice-Cream and Sabayon

制作者 李伟强 徐高治

原料 Ingredient

大芒果 Mango

君度橙酒 Cointreau Orange Liquor

香草冰激凌 Vanilla Ice-cream

鸡蛋 Egg

糖 Sugar

制作 Proceed

(1) 将芒果切成指甲大的芒果丁,用少许君度酒泡5分钟。

Soak the diced mango in Cointreau liquor for 5 minutes.

(2) 将鸡蛋放入不锈钢盆中,加入糖隔火打发后倒入君度酒成沙巴翁汁。

Foam the eggs with sugar in a hot stainless steel pot. Add Cointreau liquor in to become sabayon.

(3) 将芒果放入杯中,再放上香草冰激凌,最后淋上沙巴翁汁。

Put the mango into a cup, topped with vanilla ice-ream. Finally pour sabayon in.

178. 香蕉巴菲配梅汁 Banana Parfait with Plum Juice

制作者 李伟强 徐高治

原料 Ingredient

香蕉肉 Banana

鲜奶油 Fresh Cream

蛋黄 Egg Yolk

梅 Plum Juice

糖 Sugar

制作 Proceed

(1) 蛋黄加入糖隔水打发。

Foam the egg yolk with sugar in a hot pot.

(2) 香蕉肉打成泥。

Make the banana mud.

(3) 鲜奶油打至七至八成发。

Foam the fresh cream to 70−80 per.

(4) 将上述原料加入梅汁和酒拌匀。

Mix the ingredient in (1),(2),(3) with plum juice and wine to get sauce.

(5) 放入模具后,在零下 22℃冰柜中冰冻成型。

Pour the sauce into the mold, to become formed at −22 ℃ freezer.

179. 巧克力蛋糕配水果及白兰地 Chocolate Cake with Fruit and Brandy

制作者 李伟强 徐高治

原料 Ingredient

苦巧克力 Chocolate

黄油 Butter

全蛋 Egg

糖 Sugar

香草棒 Vanilla Bar

豆蔻粉 Nutmeg

玉桂粉 Cinnamon

制作 Proceed

(1) 将苦巧克力化开加入黄油后,再加入豆蔻粉及玉桂粉。

Put the butter in the melted chocolate. And add nutmeg, cinnamon in.

(2) 蛋黄加入香草棒及糖打发。蛋白加入糖打发。

Foam the egg yolk with vanilla bar and sugar. And foam egg white with sugar.

(3) 将上述原料拌匀加入化好的苦巧克力。

Mix the ingredient in (1) and (2) to get the sauce.

(4) 倒入模具烤制成型,配上时令水果和白兰地。

Pour the sauce into the mold to bake forming.Arrange the cake on a plate, served with Seasonal Fruit and Brandy.

180. 龙井茶面包配柠檬 Longjing Tea Bread Served with Lemon

制作者 李伟强 徐高治

原料 Ingredient

面包粉 Bread Powder

盐 Salt

鲜酵母 Fresh Yeast

温水 Warm Water

糖 Sugar

橄榄油 Olive Oil

龙井茶叶 Longjing Tea Leaves

柠檬 Lemon

香蕉 Banana

制作 Proceed

(1) 将龙井茶叶与橄榄油搅打成汁。

Whip Longjing tea leaves and olive oil as juice.

(2) 用温水把鲜酵母化开，与面包粉调匀。

Melt fresh yeast with warm water, add bread powder,and stir them.

(3) 将上述原料混合搅拌，稍后加入切碎的茶叶。

Mix the ingredcent in (1) and (2) to blend, then add chopped tea to get the sauce.

(4) 倒入模具烘制成面包，配上柠檬、香蕉。

Pour the sauce into the mold to roast.Arrange the bread on a plate, served with Lemon and banana.

181. 三文鱼太太佐鹌鹑蛋和鱼子酱 Salmon Tartar with Quail Eggs and Caviar

制作者 陆勤松

原料 Ingredient

三文鱼 Salmon
水瓜柳 Capers
红洋葱 Red Onion
橄榄油 Olive Oil
金酒 Gin
鹌鹑蛋 Quail Egg
黑鱼子酱 Black Caviar
酥皮条 Pastry
混合生菜 Mixed Lettuce
柠檬油醋汁 Lemon Oil Dressing

制作 Proceed

(1) 三文鱼用水瓜柳、红洋葱、橄榄油以及金酒、盐和胡椒调味。

Season the salmon with capers, red onion, olive oil, gin, salt and pepper.

(2) 将三文鱼装入圆形模具烤制,上放鱼子酱和鹌鹑蛋。

Put the seasoned salmon into round mold to bake, topped with the caviar and quail eggs.

(3) 将烤制好的三文鱼装盆,四周放混合生菜,淋上柠檬油醋汁。

Arrange the cooked salmon on a plate, garnished with the mixed lettuce, and sprinkled with lemon oil dressing.

182. 火焰鱼子酱和牛芝士卷 Flame Caviar and Beef Cheese Roll

制作者 陆勤松

原料 Ingredient

和牛 Japanese Beef Meat

芝士 Cheese

黑鱼子酱 Black Caviar

索甸酒 Sauternes Wine

大豆卵磷脂 Soybean Lecithin

吉哩片 Gel sheet

制作 Proceed

(1) 把芝士条、鱼子酱、芝麻菜卷入和牛片中。

Fold the Japanese beef filet with cheese stick, caviar, sesame vegetables in roll.

(2) 涂上日本酱油,用喷火枪喷烹至和牛卷七分熟。

Coat the beef roll with Japanese soy sauce, then cook it with flamethrower to medium well.

(3) 和牛卷切成三段,上放索甸酒泡沫,佐酒冻。

Cut the beef roll into three sections, topped with Sauternes wine foam, served with wine jelly.

183. 红毛蟹配野菌和松露芝士 Japanese Red Crab with Wild Mushrooms and Truffle Cheese

制作者 陆勤松

原料 Ingredient

红毛蟹 Red Crab
芝士 Cheese
奶油 Butter
黑松露油 Black Truffle Oil
混合菌菇 Mixed Mushrooms

制作 Proceed

(1) 炒菌菇，上放蟹肉，用芦笋、松露、鱼子酱做装饰。
Fried mushrooms, topped with crab meat, garnished with asparagus, truffles and caviar.

(2) 淋上用奶油、芝士、松露油制成的沙司。
Sprinkle the sauce made from cream, cheese and truffle oil.

184.香煎鲜贝配柑橘酱 Fried Fresh Scallop Served with Citrus Sauce

制作者 陆勤松

原料 Ingredient

鲜贝 Fresh Scallop

脆米粒 Grain of Rice

鱼露 Fish Sauce

橙汁 Orange Juice

粥 Porridge

黄油 Butter

青豆 Green Beans

制作 Proceed

(1) 黄油煎鲜贝。

Fry fresh scallop by butter.

(2) 用鱼露、橙汁和白米粥做成汁。

Make sauce with fish sauce, orange juice and porridge.

(3) 装盆并用炒青豆做点缀。

Arrange the food on a plate, garnished with fried green beans.

185. 牛肝菌炒龙虾佐清酒泡沫 Fried Lobster with Boletus Served with Sake Foam

制作者 陆勤松

原料 Ingredient

牛肝菌 Boletus
小青龙 Small Lobster
黄油 Butter
白葡萄酒 White Wine
柠檬汁 Lemon Juice
清酒 Sake

制作 Proceed

(1) 用黄油炒小青龙段，加入牛肝菌、青豆，以白葡萄酒、柠檬汁调味。

Fry the small lobster with butter, add boletus and peas, seasoned with white wine and lemon juice.

(2) 用清酒泡沫做点缀。

Arrange the food on a plate, garnished with sake foam.

186. 堂煎明虾佐脆火腿和海藻汁 Backed Prawn Served with Ham and Seaweed Sauce

制作者 陆勤松

原料 Ingredient

大明虾 Large Prawns

意大利火腿 Italian Ham

蟹味菇 Crab Flavor Mushrooms

青豆 Peas

牛肝菌 Boletus

黄油 Butter

柠檬汁 Lemon Juice

海藻汁 Seaweed Sauce

制作 Proceed

(1) □大明虾,加入黄油和柠檬汁调味。

Bake the large prawns, add butter and lemon juice seasoning.

(2) 炒香蟹味菇、牛肝菌和青豆。

Saute the crab flavor mushrooms, boletus and peas.

(3) 淋上黄油、虾汁和海藻沙司。

Arrange the food on a plate, sprinkled with butter, prawn sauce and seaweed sauce.

187. 煎鸭胸配鸭肉春卷 Fried Duck Breast Served with Duck Spring Rolls

制作者 陆勤松

原料 Ingredient

鸭胸 Duck Breast
榛果仁 Hazelnuts
红菜头 Beetroot
柿子 Persimmon
五香粉 Spice Powder
鸭肉春卷 Duck Spring Rolls
欧洲防风根 Opopanax

制作 Proceed

(1) 煎鸭胸至六分熟,切成方块,上面放果仁碎、红菜柿子卷。

Fry the duck breast to medium well. Arrange the diced duck on a plate, topped with the hazelnuts, beetroot and persimmon.

(2) 把鸭肉春卷放在欧洲防风根泥上。

Put the duck spring rolls on the opopanax mud.

(3) 鸭肉四周淋上沙司、罗勒装饰。

Sprinkle sauce around the duck, garnished with basil.

188. 鹅肝牛排配火腿 Goose Liver and Steak Served with Ham

制作者 陆勤松

原料 Ingredient

澳洲牛柳 Australian Beef
鹅肝 Goose Liver
蜂蜜 Honey
美国辣椒汁 American Chili Sauce
牛肉汁 Beef Juice
意大利火腿 Italian Ham
芦笋 Asparagus

制作 Proceed

(1) 煎牛柳块至六分熟,上放鹅肝。
Fry the beef to medium well, topped with goose liver.

(2) 混合蜂蜜、辣椒汁和牛肉汁。
Mix honey, chili sauce and beef juice.

(3) 佐火腿片和芦笋并装盆。
Arrange the food on a plate, served with ham and asparagus.

189. 提拉米苏沙巴杨配热带鲜果 Sabah Yang Tiramisu with Tropical Fruits

制作者 陆勤松

原料 Ingredient

马斯卡波芝士 Masikabo Cheese

马莎拉酒 MarSara Wine

蛋黄 Egg Yolk

糖圈 Sugar Ring

热带鲜果 Tropical Fruits

制作 Proceed

(1) 将芝士、马莎拉酒和蛋黄打至发泡，装入糖圈中。

Whip cheese, MarSara wine and egg yolk foaming. Pour it into sugar ring.

(2) 配上热带鲜果。

Arrange the rings on a plate, served with tropical fruits.

190. 红菜头冰淇淋配双味慕斯 Beetroot Ice-Cream with Double-Flavored Mousse

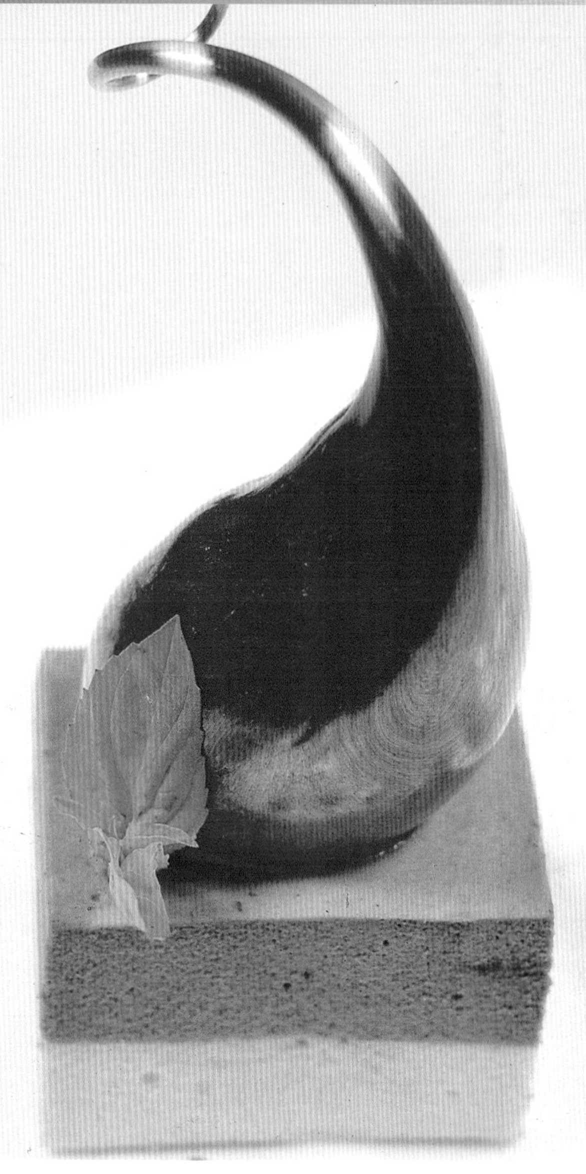

制作者 陆勤松

原料 Ingredient

红菜头 Beetroot

糖 Sugar

椰浆 Coconut milk

口哩片 Jelly Pieces

制作 Proceed

(1) 用红菜汁在冰淇淋机中制成红菜头冰淇淋。

Make beetroot ice-cream with machine.

(2) 把红菜头冰淇淋装入糖艺中。

Put the beetroot ice-cream into sugar sculpture.

(3) 加热椰浆和红菜汁,放入口哩片。

Heat coconut milk and beetroot juice, add jelly pieces.

(4) 把冰淇淋糖艺放在慕斯上并装盆。

Put the sculpture on two-flavored mousse, and arrange the plate.